D1006728

BEIRUT HELLFIRE

SOCIETY

BEIRUT
HELLFIRE
SOCIETY

A NOVEL

RAWI HAGE

W. W. Norton & Company
Independent Publishers Since 1923
New York | London

Beirut Hellfire Society is a work of fiction. Names, characters, and incidents are the products of the author's imagination or are used fictitiously. Any resemblance to actual persons, living or dead, is entirely coincidental.

Copyright © 2018 by Rawi Hage
First American Edition 2019

For information about permission to reproduce selections
from this book, write to Permissions, W. W. Norton & Company, Inc.,
500 Fifth Avenue, New York, NY 10110

For information about special discounts for bulk purchases,
please contact W. W. Norton Special Sales at
specialsales@wwnorton.com or 800-233-4830

Manufacturing by Worzalla

Library of Congress Cataloging-in-Publication Data

Names: Hage, Rawi, author.
Title: Beirut Hellfire Society : a novel / Rawi Hage.
Description: First American edition. | New York : W. W. Norton &
    Company, 2019.
Identifiers: LCCN 2018056753 | ISBN 9781324002918 (hardcover)
Subjects: LCSH: Lebanon—History—Civil War, 1975–1990—Fiction. |
    Secret societies—Fiction. | GSAFD: Historical fiction. | War stories.
Classification: LCC PR9199.4.H33 B45 2019 | DDC 813/.6—dc23
LC record available at https://lccn.loc.gov/2018056753

W. W. Norton & Company, Inc.
500 Fifth Avenue, New York, N.Y. 10110
www.wwnorton.com

W. W. Norton & Company Ltd.
15 Carlisle Street, London W1D 3BS

1 2 3 4 5 6 7 8 9 0

In memory of John Asfour

To lay my dearest brother in the grave.

—Antigone

PROLOGUE

O ne sunny day at the start of a ceasefire, a father drove
with his son down towards where the fighting had been.

A cadaver had been lying on the ground for days, mutilated. The son, who was named Pavlov, and his father, an
undertaker, loaded the remains into plastic bags and carried
them to the hearse. The cadaver's belly had been opened by
a bullet wound and vermin had claimed it and multiplied
inside the soft organs, gorging on the entrails. Father and son
gathered the scattered items that belonged to the dead: a loose
shoe, a bag filled with mouldy food, broken glasses.

Now, the man told his son, you're sixteen—old enough
to become a member of the Society. The Hellfire Society, the
father added. He switched on the car radio, and drove towards
the coast and then up into the mountains of Lebanon.

They arrived at a secluded area in the high summit, and
finally at a small stone house that looked to be abandoned. But
the father picked up a key from under a potted plant, opened
the door, and together he and his son entered. The house was
simple and humble, cold and damp. Neglect and dust could
be seen everywhere. The floor was bare, and through the soles
of their shoes father and son felt the touch of leather against
grains of dirt and sand. Walking across the room was slippery

but manageable—two pairs of feet grinding little particles into the floor. The walls of the house were peeling, exposing straw mixed with clay, an ancient technique for efficient insulation that the villagers had used for centuries. There was a bed in the corner of the main room and, in the middle, a stove with a chimney that extended its charcoal tube towards the ceiling before the cylinder shifted at the end, a perfect ninety degrees, to reach the top of the adjacent wall and cough out its smoke.

Welcome to the Society's mansion, the father said.

Pavlov followed his father into the second room. This was a later addition to the house, separate from the main area. Its cement floor was bare and unpolished and the room's main feature was a large metal door in the centre of the back wall, with a smaller door beneath the large one. Beside the doors, two large gas tanks were linked by tubes. To Pavlov's eye, they resembled the garden hoses often seen trailing like serpents around villagers' houses.

Eventually we may have to change the pipes, his father said. It's a simple procedure. You make sure to cut off the gas from its source there—he pointed at a handle embedded in the wall—and before you proceed, lock it firm. Look here, son. You twist this knob on the top in a counter-clockwise motion. Are you cold, son?

Pavlov nodded.

In no time this house will burn like hell, his father replied, and smiled. But let's eat first, and then we'll bring our unknown soul into the abode of fire, light and eternal warmth.

They washed their hands with cracked bars of soap under cold water, then roasted chestnuts, heated bread, set out thyme and olive oil and cheese that the father removed from a jar, and drank alcohol. When they were done, they brought the body inside, laid it on a wooden stretcher that the father had made himself and carried the cadaver to the second room. The father opened the metal door and Pavlov saw what looked like a deep, long oven.

The father turned to the cadaver, and with a singing, wailing voice he uttered these words: They say ashes to ashes, but we say fire begets fire. May your fire join the grand luminosity of the ultimate fire, may your anonymity add to the greatness of the hidden, the truthful and the unknown. You, the father continued, were trapped, lost, ignored, dejected, but now you are found, and we release you back into your original abode. Happy are those rejected by the burial lots of the ignorant. The earth is winter and summer, spring and fall . . . We heard your call and we came.

Father and son lifted the bed off the stretcher and slid the cadaver into the stove. The father twisted the knobs of the gas tanks—bonbons he called them—struck a match and lit a fire inside. Then he asked his son to close the furnace door.

In time, the house became warm. It stood alone in its surroundings, a ball of heat against the chill of the mountains. Pavlov, bewildered by the rituals, sat in silence and listened as his father talked and drank and sang incomprehensible songs that had the rhythms of hymns. Then his father, drunk and tired, stumbled into bed and fell asleep.

Pavlov stayed awake and gazed at the wooden stove, watching the glow of a few persistent coals coating themselves in grey dust on the outside, burning red and orange at the core. Heat percolated from the second room, so strong it made Pavlov loosen his wool coat and remove his socks and extend his toes. He studied the downcast moustache drawing a line around his father's open mouth below a triangular Byzantine nose, long and curved, and thin at its tip. Pavlov wondered about the singing, and about the burning of stray corpses, unclaimed and bloated, about orphaned cadavers and their capacity for music and dance long lost. *My father has done this before, alone.* What strength, Pavlov thought, what willpower must have been required to lift the heavy bodies and load them into the car. Pavlov examined his father's shoulders, strong from digging the earth and carrying hardened, blue bodies; and his father's fingers, infiltrated by dust beneath the nails. From the balcony at home, Pavlov had often seen his father digging, and waving to him when he straightened to stretch his back, and drinking water from the bottle at his side. Tonight's long, esoteric monologue and affectionate words made Pavlov wonder if his father was addressing him or some other distant son, or if he was simply filled with life and liquor. The incoherent speeches about death, ephemerality, the *Iliad*'s fallen heroes, and quotes from various saints and philosophers from Heraclitus to Ephrem the Syrian; the disquisitions on ancient burials, fire, and epics from antiquity; and the disdain for the earth, the body . . . it all made Pavlov wonder if his father might be a madman, a deranged heathen. All these years, he had thought his father's criticism of the clergy was because the priests meddled in matters of burial grounds and money. Now he realized that his father disliked earthly burials on principle. He preferred fire.

And then his father woke, and liberating the words inside him, told his son that he dearly wished he could have burned his wife, Pavlov's mother, when she had died a few months past—but she had insisted on being buried in the ground, and he had respected her wish. As for myself, the father said, you, my son, will bring me fire.

Pavlov looked at his father again and saw a gentle, eccentric man, and he pitied him and loved him all the more.

—

At dawn, the father woke the son, gathered ashes from the furnace, mixed them with water, and pasted them all over his face and hands.

Pavlov brushed his teeth and washed his face, and went to stand outside beside his father. He was both embarrassed and filled with wonder. It was cold that morning—the cold of soldiers marching towards battle, stomping across farmers' fields, cold in the way vengeful villagers steal dead soldiers' shoes after defeat in battle, cold like that rosy dawn in which the wounded trip over vegetables, roots and dead branches, bruised, shot, stabbed and hallucinating of a wedding with a farmer's girl who will lead them towards their warrior heaven. Pavlov looked at the vast empty mountains while his father chanted. Then his father kissed Pavlov on the forehead, took his hand and led him in another dance, singing in a foreign language. Pavlov danced and smiled, bewildered but surrendering to his father's wishes and following his steps.

Afterwards, he helped gather the ashes from the crematorium and fold them in a cloth. The two of them walked along a narrow path, through bushes and between tall, prehistoric rocks until they reached a cliff that looked out onto a steep valley. The view was sublime and the wind passed over them, just as it had passed over the succession of round green hills and into the valley. Pavlov's father flipped the cloth open, and the ashes were taken by the wind and the dust scattered in one direction. The northern wind, his father said, leads south, and the easterly wind leads west and carries with it the scent of time.

Inside the house, his father washed his hands and face, dried them with a cloth, fed the cloth into the stove in the middle of the room and let it burn.

Then father and son drove back to the city of Beirut, once more they drove, in silence under the falling bombs. The war had resumed.

BEIRUT,
1978

SPRING

AT THE WINDOW

The man who had been given the name Pavlov by his father stood at his window above the road that led to the cemetery, and waited for the bells to toll. Upon hearing that sound, he swallowed his saliva and settled in to watch the procession going by.

Women in black gowns dragged their ponderous heels on the unpaved road, and men in sombre colours shortened, with their breath, white cigarettes trapped between their scissor-like fingers and lead-filled teeth. Pavlov recognized a few of the men, despite their newly sad faces and their hunched shoulders that reminded him of hungry dogs on their way to disposal bins behind the city's restaurants and butcher shops.

He watched as one of the neighbourhood's two clergy-men performed the burial ceremonies. Since his birth, for twenty years, he had witnessed the traffic of floating caskets passing under his prominent nose, and he could predict the priests' repetitive movements, recite their chants by heart, smell the swinging incense burners chained like dogs on leashes as the priests recited prayers over bones and caskets. The clergymen's long black robes, carefully trimmed just above the ankles, avoided the dust that rose from beneath their shoes.

Upon the sight of either priest, Pavlov would look at the floor and curse the hour of the man's birth. He blamed the ancient Egyptians for these masquerades, for the invention of priesthood and its deep power. He also cursed the Platonic "junta"—as he referred to the Neoplatonic philosophers— for preaching the transmigration of souls.

Everyone aspires to end as a king—a dead king. His father had said these words only last year, on his most recent trip with Pavlov to the cremation site on the mountain.

Pavlov lived alone with his father in a two-storey house above the cemetery road. His sister had eloped six years ago with a butcher who lived high in the mountains. She had despised the passage of the dead in their coffins beneath the family's front window. Their mother, who had died soon after Pavlov turned sixteen, was buried in the cemetery across from the house. After his sister's departure and his mother's illness and death, Pavlov had become the custodian of the window of death, the sole observer above the cemetery road.

Down below, the passage of coffins was a ritual watched by everyone in the neighbourhood except Pavlov's father the undertaker, and his father's two brothers, the assistant under-takers, who would wait by the grave, hosts at the bedside of the open earth.

Now, standing at the window, Pavlov reached for his box of cigarettes and arbitrarily withdrew one by the tip of its beak. He contemplated the rebirth of ashes inside its rolled and flaming paper. Fire, Pavlov thought. How fond his father was of fire. His father would occasionally mention the mysterious Society that was somehow connected with fire, but Pavlov still did not know exactly what it was. And since Pavlov had never met anyone else from this elusive society, he believed it must be yet another of his father's eccentric fables, or part of some esoteric religious liturgy that his father would mutter when no one but Pavlov was present, or in the presence of the dead.

This world, my son, he would tell Pavlov, was created by a lesser God. The true God, the God of light, is beyond the realm of this demeaning world. And when he washed the dead, Pavlov's father would utter words both of love and of disdain. Oh, this body of yours, he would say to the cadaver, this entrapment of filth and a handful of light. He would sometimes dance, and sometimes sing, and on a few occasions Pavlov had even seen him cry.

Over the past few years Pavlov had learned to perfectly time his cigarette. He smoked and looked at the horizon to avoid seeing the clergymen walk by, mumbling to himself, mocking them. By the third or fourth puff, wailing women would have reached the corner of his house, and that was when the men in the procession would turn and signal to the women to halt and not continue to the cemetery. The descent of the casket would be witnessed only by the men, as the norms of this ancient Christian community dictated. But once in a while a persistent sister or mother would rush towards the metal gate and try to rescue her loved one before the mudhole swallowed the remains beneath the men's black ties and the sealing shovels of the gravediggers. Pavlov would watch these renegade women from his window. Some would grab the metal bars of the cemetery gate and beg for their loved one's resurrection before falling on their knees and weeping in acceptance, and slowly fading into silence. Others would scream and challenge the gods, *Prove you really exist. I am going to close my eyes and count to three and you will bring my child back here!*

Pavlov knew the sound of bells was the cruellest thing the relatives of the dead would endure in the days after a burial. He felt a perverse privilege in watching the mourning daughters, sisters and mothers pass underneath his window. He cried at the sight of their beauty. Death and tears, he thought—that's what it takes for this world to be made humble. He blamed his sentimentality on his religious upbringing. The aesthetic of sadness that his tribe had perfected was something conditioned into his being, and certainly the location of his house, and the repetitive migrations of death beneath his window, had through the years engraved in him a love of tragic beauty.

Men and women he recognized from his long years of captivity in his insular neighbourhood were transformed on this path into howling bodies. The women's elegant black dresses and the tears appearing on their cheeks like morning dew seemed to him to be the most truthful expression of his world. It was the little white handkerchiefs that always got him—cloth that must be the gifts of mysterious lovers, he fancied. Black handkerchiefs, on the other hand, he imagined to be self-acquired, as they were usually owned by the older women for whom these romantic gestures no longer held the same hope; their greying heads had passed along these roads before, and utilitarian ornaments such as handkerchiefs and hairpins and black stockings had become part of life's necessities. During times of burial, phrases emerged from these women in short bursts, sentences that referenced the most mundane recollections of their loved ones: *I cooked that dish today . . . The radio is still on . . . My sweet such-and-such said to me yesterday . . . The neighbour prepared food and we waited . . .*

Pavlov observed, from his position as spectator of death, that no matter how tragic their beloved's demise, in times of burial these women never laid direct blame on the killers or on the brutality of life, or on war for that matter. Nor did they blame rulers or deities. What remained with them were these fragmented memories of daily repetitive gestures. He saw that women, in gathering close to death, were in these times of mourning the producers of a most unique symphony, a collective weeping that had evolved into one of mankind's most sophisticated chants. It was often initiated by a non-member of the clan, one who nonetheless considered herself part of the deceased's family. The instinctive harmony, Pavlov theorized, must have evolved over the millennia of loss and death that every species endures before its inevitable, eventual extinction. Perhaps the women's chorus of grief was an attempt to prevent further deaths, which, in a time of burial, would certainly be catastrophic and result in great disorder. Or so Pavlov imagined as he smoked and watched.

After the procession was over, he would retreat to his bedroom, drop the cigarette on the floor, step on it, lie down on his bed, loosen his tie and liberate himself from the burden of cloth and thread. Then he would pull an old book from his father's library and, naked, light a cigarette and read through the night.

THREE BOMBS

The undertakers were busier than ever.

Beirut had been bombed for days on end and the road to the cemetery hosted three or four processions a day. Some mourners went to the graveyard and then came back to stand under Pavlov's balcony, waiting for the next procession to arrive so they could join the march again. Men stood around and smoked and talked about everything and anything except death and the deceased while Pavlov assisted his father and his uncles, digging up the ground in profound rectangular shapes, driving the hearse back and forth, cleaning and beautifying the dead, and burying them.

On a sunny Sunday, as Pavlov's two uncles were praying with their families in church and his father was readying the earth for the next burial, three bombs were fired towards the east side of the city. They gathered in the air, suspended, indecisive, assessing their targets, and for a fraction of a second they formed a trinity witnessed only by Pavlov, the man whose name declared his preference for dogs over humans.

The first bomb headed for the city's port, flying above the concrete buildings with vicious velocity, and above reception aerials, to the bewilderment of the local TV anchors and the amusement of cartoon characters pounding each other inside their small glass screens. It looked down on the cement houses, water tanks and pigeon coops on the rooftops, down on the residents cooking in their Teflon non-stick pots, then made its way to the French stairs that linked the little hill of Achrafieh to the lower part of the neighbourhood of Gemmayze, where the houses are more elaborate, with their Ottoman and Florentine architecture, their large tripartite arched windows dominating their facades and hosting morning sunlight that struck directly the chain-smoker inhabitants fanning their long eyelashes to chase away the fumes escaping their nostrils and the ash landing on their outrageously tailored dresses, carbon copies of the garments in French fashion magazines found in dentists' offices or sold by bored merchants confined to kiosk cigarette counters with displays of lottery tickets and relentless chewing gum, gum bought and pulped by the wisdom teeth of women in hairdressing salons toasting their painted heads in spherical dryers that resembled the helmets of alien visitors in B-rated movies, visitors from outer space. Bombs or no bombs, I am fixing my hair, said a woman named Marie, and I am having a pedicure and a manicure. I refuse to look like a maid. War or no war, I'll pull back my husband's eye if it wanders sideways or upwards to the apartment of that whore Evelyne Khoury who shows her inner thighs through the balcony bars and advertises her grand tits between the open casements. Moi, cherie, j'aime pas les chrameets, et Evelyne est une charmoutah. How I hate her!

This first bomb disregarded the Electric Company building, missed the tower of a little Armenian church and headed down towards the seaside, where it whizzed over the head of a grocer engrossed by the expiry dates on canned food and exhausted by the talk of war in the newspapers, finally to land on the port's plateau where containers carried by faraway ships were deposited on transit ground, destined for the deserted planets of the Gulf and for the newly oil-rich to gorge themselves on French liqueurs, perfume, extravagant cars and entertaining appliances, indulging a stupefying taste for Western modernity that would surely afford them a higher status. The bomb killed two Nazarene men who were stealing goods from blown-out opened-up containers at the port, and another man in his thirties who was later described as long-haired, wearing a long robe like a woman, with filthy feet in Roman sandals, and who stood in the open harbour space mumbling to himself words of wrath and forgiveness. The bomb left the long-haired man intact except for a wound below his left ribcage and a few holes in his palms and feet, but these wounds prevented him from carrying away any of the stolen goods, or eating the candies or gum that kept on slipping through the hole in his palm as the missiles kept falling.

The second bomb landed in the populous neighbourhood of Karm el-Zeitoun, on a barbershop, and claimed five lives. All of the victims were retired men, some living off their sons who sent money from abroad, some apt to wander around in their night pyjamas as if challenging the daytime that only brought them war and misery. All five gathered every morning at the same time for a coffee at the barbershop and to speculate on politics and posture before the oval glass, prophesying on bets and on racehorses. All of the men died, but the barber, who happened to be in the backroom boiling the morning Arabic coffee, survived. The barber did not blame himself for the massacre, but he would never again touch a cup of coffee after the incident and gave free haircuts on the sidewalk outside the shell of his old shop until his death a few weeks later.

The third bomb swirled twice around the church bell and rushed to the densely populated side of a small neighbourhood laden with cars and little shops. It froze, then suddenly changed direction and aimed towards the quiet side of the cemetery. It landed at the far end, where a gravedigger, shovel in hand, had been standing above a rectangular hole in the ground, contemplating the horizontal dimensions of the stiff whose coffin he would later lay to rest. The gravedigger was sweating, perhaps from the high sun that fell upon the city that day.

The bomb landed at his side, interrupting the methodical rhythm of his shovelling, leaving unanswered the question of whether he had any final tune in his head, or if he realized at that moment the irony of his own death while part of him fell into his own man-made pit.

The man's son, Pavlov, who happened to be standing at the window of the adjacent house, giving him a clear view of the cemetery grounds, looked for his father after the smoke had cleared, but couldn't see him. He rushed to rescue his father's remains, but there was little left to gather. Most of the body was found in the pit, but some parts were scattered on graves and headstones and in the trees.

In this way, Pavlov lost both his parents.

His father was reburied a few days later, beside his mother—despite Pavlov's quiet objection to his sister and his uncles. One of his uncles added his father's name to the headstone and sealed the argument. The night of that burial day, Pavlov brought a light to his cigarette and laid the burning cylinder on top of the grave. A temporary fire, he whispered to his father. One day, when the time is right, I'll exhume your body and burn it, and offer your ashes to the wind.

POSSESSIONS

A short while later, Pavlov's sister Nathalie drove with her husband Joseph back to the city. They came with their little daughter, dragging their muddy, heavy villagers' shoes up the stairs of the family home. And when they reached Pavlov's door, they peeped inside before entering. They paused and looked, pretending to catch their breath from the conquest of the stairs, wondering what had changed in the house in their long absence, what had been added or subtracted. Then they sighed in the knowledge that nothing had changed. Everything was the same, except that Pavlov's father had now removed himself from the company of the furniture.

The husband, Joseph, indifferent and reluctant, but dragged forwards by his wife and by all the inadequacy that hung off the tip of his married man's nose, like a big bull dragged by a ring that alternated between his middle finger and his painful-as-if-pierced nostrils, hung his head and took a deep breath, filling his gigantic chest with the city's pathological air of bronchospasms, sewers, fossil fuels and body odours. Like a Mongol invader, he feared and scorned cities. For the first fifteen years of his life, he had never seen one. His closest encounters with cities were the city folk who arrived in his village of Kfaroumeh on summer holidays. They looked odd to him, arrogant women, men who spoke like singers on the radio. They drove their cars heedlessly, never stopping to greet anyone, never looking you in the eye, and if you happened to be walking they would never stop to offer a lift. But in his wife he had found both aloofness and humility. Though a city girl, she always seemed like a villager to him, humble yet assertive. She loved the village and the people in the village loved her. But she kept her father's profession a secret. When asked, she would answer: My father ploughs for a living.

Pavlov's sister and her husband took everything modern, utilitarian and functional in the house: kitchenware, quilts, furniture and clothes. They took all that they could carry, packing it up with the rush of thieves during a riot. Their energy seemed to rise with the weight of the goods in their hands. And they proclaimed their gratitude for gravity: descending is easier, they said, even with a weight in your arms; it's going up that is hard. They stated the obvious and took the obvious, leaving Pavlov with the various objects his father had collected from dead loners who'd had no one to mourn them— rifles or paintings or cameras, diverse objects that lay unmoved by quiet endings.

Pavlov's father had been a hoarder of death's memorabilia; he'd collected everything and anything the dead no longer had any use for. Those who couldn't afford burials had paid him in paintings, old magazines, books, vases and stamp collections. Those who had died without heirs had their belongings and jewellery brought home. Once in a while, his father would bring home the unclaimed cadaver of a vagrant from under a bridge, an old person who had lived alone with no one to account for them, wanderers, outlaws, dead foreign workers trapped in a land of war where no money was available to repatriate them. When Pavlov had reached his thirteenth birthday, his father began to take him along to pick up "orphaned bodies," as his father called them. He would hand Pavlov gloves and a mask, and they would collect the dead and bring the body to the funeral home. His father would keep the anonymous corpse for a day or two, clean it and dress it, and then he would disappear with it overnight, all by himself, and come back the following morning. When Pavlov asked where he had gone, his father would reply, A meeting with the Society.

Nathalie and Joseph ignored the paintings, the antiques, the diaries of the dead, the mittens and the old church ladies' scarves, the rosaries, the drawers filled with knick-knacks and photo albums, the elaborate hats, the canes, vases, false teeth and medicinal ivory boxes, the Roman busts and Turkish vases, the jade, the old books and English china. They took the large carpets and left the small ones to Pavlov. They took the sofas, the dressers and massive wooden armoires, the mirror with its heavy frame. And his sister, before she got into

her butcher husband's truck, said to Pavlov, Sell the house
and come live with us.

But Pavlov refused. I like it here, he said.

And what do you like about it? his sister cried angrily.

The view, he said, and gave her a small smile.

You stay here among the dead, then. I am going back to
the country, to a place where everything is always alive.

Nothing is alive forever, Pavlov said.

Oh, you and your Greeks, Nathalie replied. And she
climbed into the truck and sat beside her husband, holding
another box in her hands.

The butcher was quiet. He was only half-literate, and
had a dolichocephalic head, and it seemed to Pavlov as if his
red cheeks must have, through the years, absorbed the colours
of the bare flesh he assaulted and divided in his little shop.
His hands were thick, so unlike the curiously delicate hands
of Pavlov's father, the undertaker and mortician who fancied
himself a surgeon or the owner of a beauty parlour special-
izing in red nails, platitudes and neighbourhood gossip. I
guess, Pavlov thought, the butcher's hands that profit from
taking apart the dead need to be stronger than the hands of
a man who decorates them.

NADJA

After his sister's departure, Pavlov stayed alone at home for a long while. He lingered on his balcony, he gazed at the night sky. He smoked. He turned on the transistor radio and walked back to the balcony to join his drink before the alcohol evaporated or was swallowed by some wandering spirit from the underground. Sometimes he caught a tune from the radio and slowly swayed and eventually danced. He moved with a twitch in his eye, dodging the smoke from the cigarette migrating between his lip and the tips of his fingers. He danced for the sun scuttling down towards Hades. He thought of the Greeks again, he thought of Helen standing by the walls of Troy in the company of a king, gesticulating and lamenting warriors' deaths. He did his reverse dance, turning his back to the window and the world, gazing at the last luminosity on the wall inside the house, reciting the *Iliad*, a book that he had read again and again in both his youth and his adulthood, imagining the crosses across the road in the cemetery turning into spears, and mourners' prayers into battle cries, and captive Helen looking down from the Trojan wall.

And then he thought of Nadja, a prostitute who had come to visit his father one night, in the company of two of her friends, to bury a third friend who had been killed by her captor.

This was a night long after his mother's death and his sister's departure. Three women had knocked on his father's door and walked up the stairs in their high heels, their blond hair loose on their shoulders. The Society had sent them, they said, and his father had offered them coffee. Then he said, I'll come with my son to pick up your loved one.

Come late at night, they told Pavlov's father. And they arranged to meet him on a side street.

Pavlov had listened closely to Nadja as she explained everything to his father in a heavy French accent. Then she turned to her co-workers and switched into a foreign language that Pavlov imagined to be Trojan Greek.

When his father asked Pavlov to escort the ladies back downstairs, Pavlov walked ahead with a torch in hand, and at the bottom of the staircase he gallantly gave Nadja his hand to overcome the last step. Merci, she said, in a soft, singing tone.

He asked her if she spoke Greek.

Greek! Nadja said, and all three women laughed. No, we don't.

The next night, Pavlov and his father drove to the Naba'a neighbourhood. They passed the little bridge that linked Achrafieh to Bourj Hammoud and one of the women met them on a corner near the famous Falafel Ajax. The woman got in, and together they drove through the maze of the neighbourhood and parked the hearse in a back alley. Pavlov and his father followed the woman into a house and up the stairs.

Inside, the other two women were waiting, smoking. They looked nervous, but not sad. They also wore a look that Pavlov did not understand, perhaps one that surfaced after the presence of violence—or was it defiance he saw in their faces?

Nadja led the way to the back room.

A woman was laid out on the bed. She had been murdered. Blood covered her breast above the heart, and there were bruises on her arms and face. Pavlov's father didn't ask any questions, and after a moment the three women led him and Pavlov to another room, and opened the door. A dead man, also covered in blood, lay on the floor half-wrapped in a white sheet, a Caesar stabbed by many blades.

We killed him, Nadja said calmly and without remorse, because he killed her.

We'll take care of both, Pavlov's father said. But one at a time. The woman first. My son will come back for the man later.

Later that night, Pavlov returned. Before he took the body to the car, he and Nadja stood above the dead man and spontaneously held hands.

Then Pavlov carried the cadaver down the stairs, and Nadja followed him.

Come back and see me sometime, she said.

EL-MARQUIS VISITS PAVLOV

Pavlov heard a car advancing along the cemetery road and parking outside his home. He peeked out the window. A tall man in white, with a wide white hat, stepped out of the car and knocked at Pavlov's door.

Pavlov hurried downstairs and opened the door. The man on the step was distinguished, if perhaps on the flamboyant side. He introduced himself as El-Marquis, and said that he had been a friend of Pavlov's late father. Pavlov invited him in.

Upstairs, the man sat down on the biggest chair in the living room, smiling at Pavlov before turning his attention to the empty walls.

A minimalist, he said to Pavlov. I haven't seen any of your fine species in our country for a while.

Pavlov smiled. He was pleased by this observation. He chose a chair opposite the man in white, sat down and waited for him to speak.

As I said, I am a friend of your late father, but let me be more specific. I am one of the founders of a group we call the Hellfire Society. You may have heard of us from your father. We had great respect for him.

Pavlov nodded.

His service to us was always indispensable.

Pavlov kept his silence.

Your father was a reluctant member of our society. We had our differences, but the respect for our separate beliefs was mutual. In short, he was a believer in the deities, or perhaps one deity. The rest of us have never believed in the existence of a God. But what we had in common was our defiance of the petty rulers of this world. For the most part, we express this in our own, you might say, *libertine* ways—or, in your father's case, he expressed it with his religious conviction and rituals. We think that the body should be simultaneously celebrated and undermined, and I believe he felt the same way. He simply happened to believe in the transcendental, while we do not. Our paths crossed mostly over matters of death and burials. We paid your father for his services. Our members want to be buried outside the religious apparatus, which as you know is almost impossible in our conservative society. If you ask me, our state has managed to combine the worst of every system possible: pseudo-democracy with a deep theocratic foundation, while we pathologically live our daily existence by old feudal norms. I say that this region's theocratic attachment is its downfall, but religion was something that your father and I often disagreed about. I would argue that our libertine ways are better

suited than any religion to protect man's core against the devastating and tragic reality of life. And most of our members
want to be cremated, not "blessed" by any priest or clergy or
traditional religion. We prefer to be "sprinkled," as we called
it. Confinement is never our choice, and the box, as we in
the Society often jokingly call the coffin, is not for us. Ashes
fly, but cadavers sink and rot. Have you been to the cremation place, Mr. Pavlov?

Pavlov nodded.

I thought as much. By the way, your father did mention
you on a few occasions. As I recall, a peculiar humorous story
is attached to your name . . . about how, as a small child, you
noticed a starving dog lingering around the door of the mor-
tuary, so you reached into a scrap bucket and threw entrails
to the dog just as churchbells rang out a burial tune. Your
father described how, over the next few weeks, every time
the bells rang for a funeral the dog would appear at the door
and you would feed the creature. That's when he began to
call you Pavlov, isn't it?

Well, in any case, my dear Pavlov—if you will allow me to
drop the formalities and call you Pavlov? We in the Society
are the ones who built and paid for the crematorium that
was added to the house in the mountains. And we put your
father in charge of it. We also allowed him to use it for his own
project. We never minded his altruistic tendencies so long as
everything was kept secret.

But, dear Pavlov, allow me to tell you my life story. I present myself as a prototype for the Hellfire Society membership.
I think you will have gathered by now that we are, save your

late wonderful father, what one might call hedonists, heathens, idolaters, infidels, *Kouffar*—even, I would proudly say, happy debauchers. I personally take pride in all these defamatory labels. I routinely frequent forbidden, clandestine places and live by these liberating principles. I embrace both ways, if you know what I mean, so my appetite for bodily experiences has always been ferocious. But let me share with you a few highlights of my life. I do hope that I am not taking too much of your time. Will you tell me to stop when you need me to go?

Pavlov simply nodded again.

My dear man, I have lived the life of a libertine. From my father, I inherited a fortune. And later, through a few business endeavours along with my teaching career, I enhanced that fortune. People consider me a vain, selfish person. And I admit I am what you might call an egotistical hedonist, or at best a selfish human being—or so I have been described by former lovers, foes and friends. (Here El-Marquis was overcome, for several seconds, with laughter.) For many years I taught French literature at the Jesuit University of St. Joseph of Beirut. Educating others might well be considered a moral act of giving, but I consciously sought to corrupt the youth, and not only by the Socratic method. My pedagogical approach was different—unorthodox, if you will, and hands-on, to use the vulgar American expression. I taught my students by challenging them, conversing with them, seducing them. Yes, I slept with many of my students and colleagues, in the full knowledge that it was against the social and academic norms. Inside the Jesuit university I taught literature and history, but I believed that teaching should also take place outside of institutions, and with a good dose of intimacy. Your father told me that you are fond of the Greeks. So you must understand that the pedagogical and the sexual are not exclusive. With the Greeks, sometimes it enhanced their thought, solidarity and, consequently, their might.

El-Marquis laughed again, unleashing a deep cough that soon drove him to stand up and move to the bathroom. Pavlov heard him coughing again through the door, then spitting, and finally twisting the rusty faucets. Then El-Marquis swayed his way back to the large chair he had adorned with his hat, cigarettes and leather purse. He said, Where was I? Oh, yes.

Many of my students went on to become accomplished in their careers and to live interesting lives, and I consider that this taste of sexual liberation and close intellectual encounters was my most precious epistemological gift to the youth. I say this with utmost sincerity and humility. (He tapped his cigarette delicately on the edge of the ashtray.) I watched them flowering in my arms—male undergraduates liberated from their latent inhibitions, and young, intelligent women who suffered from the inadequacies of the younger men, who were unable to converse with or properly court these beauties, or meaningfully exchange both thought and body fluids.

Let us take as an example my past student, Florence. Florence, whom I seduced when she was just eighteen. She was *une femme-enfant*, as the French say when describing a woman who retains the charm and devious behaviour of a child. I set out to perform for her my role as a creator of wonders, histories, literatures, a student of antiquity and a teller of stories—stories of violence and love, and violence in the name of love, and love for the sake of violence, et cetera. I exposed her, as I did all my students, to the poetry of love and my love for poetry. Of course, I started by recommending books and pretending to need to meet in cafés for educational purposes. And yes, I slipped my hand between Florence's thighs after a few weeks of courting. After that I introduced her to an appreciation of wine, and the benefits of smoking hashish while reciting Baudelaire's *Fleurs du mal*. Allow me to share with you the following line from this sublime poet—and have no fear, my dear man, I have no intention of seducing you, however nice that might be: *Sur l'oreiller du mal c'est Satan Trismégiste . . .* Ah yes, this brings back memories of getting drunk in bed while reading poetry on summer days as the shouts of paddlers on the river, the screams of gamblers from down the road, the play of kids at recess in schoolyards, the occasional August breeze—all these ornaments of seduction entered our open window, and all merged with images from elsewhere, creating the necessary escape for the young and eager to learn.

To escape the war when it broke out, we impersonated Parisians and researched the names of charlatan poets who had swindled royal ladies in aristocratic salons out of food and money. I remember asking Florence if she would have slept with one of those unbathed French poets, or would have passed out from the smell of their pungent armpits and unwashed genitals coated in perfume and powder. She smiled and said, They can't be dirtier than you, and we laughed and we kissed. We would try to guess by these poets' verses who would have been the filthiest of them all. It must have been Rimbaud, she said, because he hardly ever left his bed. But he was in a closet homosexual relationship with a fellow called Paul, I said. Just imagine the perfume Paul must have enjoyed! And yes, of course, I was the one to touch her virginity, and who better than a person who has esteem for slow, penetrating thoughts and deep inquisitions of the mind? Though I realize a refined sensibility and intellectual stamina don't always translate into sensuality and good sex. But puritanism and religiosity, we both agreed, was our enemy, and how pleasurable and facile it was to disrupt it. Puritanism always destroys itself from the inside out because, for the puritan, only the exterior, that shell of morality, is washed and kept clean. Puritanism, I told Florence, is a self-serving lie created by the perverse, those who secretly long for filth.

Are you saying that all purists are masochists? she asked me.

Yes, dear, indeed, I replied. There is a deep perversity in withholding sex and pleasure. These puritans wait and wait, anticipating the most profane, cosmological, celestial orgasm. Alleluia!

At this, El-Marquis laughed loudly and coughed a little more, his madness surfacing—or was it drunkenness, Pavlov wondered, even as he enjoyed this encounter. He smoked, smiled, and listened to his visitor in white, this friend of the father Pavlov adored.

Resurrection after a long sacrifice, that's what sexual deprivation is all about, El-Marquis proclaimed, waving his cigarette in the air. Dear Florence, I said, ask yourself why these religions teach collective deprivation. I will tell you why! So that when the grand and holy orgy of Resurrection arrives from above, everyone will be so desperate that great, lustful, immortal fucking will occur, with the chattering of teeth and sweat behind the knees. Bodily fluids shall irrigate the heavens and the earth, offering bliss to agrarian cultures and thirsty saints, and pious villagers will finally get their reward in a fruitful abundance of tufted, hay-soft pubic hair. At last the meek shall be riding on the clouds of debauchery and flying horses . . . Alas, none of us in the Society will be invited—or not me, at least, because I have never deprived myself, I have never withheld . . . Oh, how greedy those puritans are, so patient and so greedy. I envy them . . . Oh, the howls . . . oh, the celestial howls . . . The open calls and the selection of wide-open orifices . . .

El-Marquis sighed, then continued.

Dear Pavlov, a revelation came to me one night when Florence mentioned the Marquis de Sade (it is from him I get my borrowed name, but I am assuming you already guessed that. Your father said that you're a reader, perhaps even a laconic, silent little scholar . . .) In any case, when the name of de Sade was evoked, it took the relationship with Florence to a different level. Sexual transgression became our way of dealing with the boredom that is so widespread in our traditional society, with its omnipresent war, its meek religiosity. Our nation lives within a culture of shaming and shame, and we decided to challenge it by committing the most daring acts of transgression.

My dear Pavlov, I had the idea to rent a small studio that sat just inside the front line. And I met with Florence in that studio. It was in the city centre and close to the Green Line, where, as you know, the most vicious battles take place. In the midst of falling bombs and fighting we would drink, and smoke the best hash in the world, and fuck for hours. The thrill of fucking in close proximity to bullets and bombs was, in my opinion, the most appropriate political act one could engage in. But our daring escalated. We started fucking at the window and watching the bombs fall, and the little bursts of smoke here and there from the bombs as they landed excited us even more. Once, on the roof, when Florence pretended to misbehave, I whipped her with a *khayzaran*, and then she turned and sucked me and stuck her finger up my ass, and later wiped it on a page of a holy book while bombs and bullets were landing and penetrating every wall and window around us. It was sublime, the emptiness—a whole city and not a single sound from any human or animal. The city's cowardly inhabitants were hiding in shelters like rats, and finally this nation of loquacious mercantile mutts was silenced. But Florence and I, my dear Pavlov, we were on the roof and close to the sky. We hoped for an encounter with a fighter who would spot us, join us or kill us . . .

But war was always one step ahead of us with its transgressions, profanity and cruelties. War is the master fucker, and no matter how we tried to degrade our bodies, war always degraded it more, and won. Its omnipotence was unsurpassable, its capacity to burn, to mutilate, was far superior to and more courageous than anything we could achieve in our fucking encounters. So what could we do but obey it and worship it? We had no choice. On a day of extreme heat, I walked to

an arms dealer and asked for a rifle with a scope. I told him
that I wanted to hunt deer, and the dealer chuckled and said,
Yeah, everyone is hunting deer these days. If you walk down
this street, there at the end of the yard, you will encounter a
large container and a few burning tires and sandbags, the kind
that deer love to chew on. Be quiet, be patient and wait, this
merchant of weapons said, laughing, and the deer will come
by. Here, take a few more packs of bullets. I'll give you a good
price and, one of these days, you'll invite me for venison stew
and a glass of arak.

The next day, Florence and I were in the rented studio.
I was inside her anus, holding the rifle at my side. I handed
the weapon to her and she aimed it in the direction of the
highway. She started shooting indiscriminately at passing
cars on distant roads. She would say, Now, and I would push
myself farther then pause my thrusting, and she would pull
the trigger on innocent drivers. Later, we would turn on the
radio to hear the news announcer warning about snipers on
that distant highway.

One day, the news reported that a man and a child had
been killed on that road. Their deaths had occurred at the same
hour when we had pulled the trigger and in the same place
where we had aimed. Florence had hit the tires of a car and it
had spun out of control and crashed into an electrical pole.
Father and son had died. The kid had flown out the window
and landed on the street.

Florence left me that same day.

She eventually married a rich man, unsurprisingly—a
bore of a businessman who was just like most men in this

dreadful, dull society. A philistine. He bought her everything and flew her everywhere because (or so I told myself) my private tuition had ended, and now she could have a life beyond these little escapades and small intellectual fantasies. She had walked away and was beyond poetry and debauchery. And of course, she could always take a sensitive, cultured lover—a poor poet maybe, to offset her mercantile, ignoramus husband—and let her husband cover the food and hotel bills out of his deep fat pockets.

Why am I telling you this, my dear?

Because today I am alive, but the next time you see me I won't be so talkative . . . I am dying soon. I am a sick man, my dear Pavlov, and I am telling you my life story because I assume that when a good story is attached to a body, that body may be treated with more liberty and less care . . . Yes, *less* care, my dear Pavlov, because after my death I want my body to become a symbol of my life.

Let's have another drink, dear Pavlov. As you may have noticed, I had a few before my arrival here. I was eager to meet you. And I am not yet done with my stories, but you seem not to mind my intrusion into your sanctuary. Thank you, dear Pavlov, and pour some more please. I trust people like you, who always have a drink to offer . . . Where was I? Well, there was Chantal, after Florence left me—Chantal, the bourgeois Christian Lebanese from the Sursock neighbourhood who went through a phase of hating her name, her religion, her class, her parents and herself. She was ashamed of her French name and her French upbringing in that local, aristocratic Lebanese milieu. Oh, my dear Pavlov, she wanted to become one with the poor, a caviar socialist. She aspired to be part of the fabric of this region, to become a lower-class Arab, *une militante*, but alas, in her travels to Paris, the few times she met young impoverished Arab men she was repulsed by their provincial manners and ignorance. She despised how they exhaled their cigarette fumes through their noses and how their open shirts exposed their chest hair and how they wore ostentatious gold rings. And then, in the month of fasting, the smell of their empty stomachs was nauseating, as were their direct sexual advances.

Still, she read Arabic literature and loved the language, and she equated being Arab with being leftist, with solidarity with the oppressed and the Palestinian cause. In Paris, she embarked on a fucking spree, screwing every young *beur* she could get her hands on. She would fuck Moroccans, Algerians, Sudanese, Yemenis. She supported them with her daddy's money, and invited them to the family apartment, to the dismay of her francophile liberal father. Her socialite mother was wary of these street boys who would steal the jewellery and the toiletries, and gorge on the contents of the fridge, chewing their food with open mouths, propping their sneaker-clad feet on the coffee table. And then, once in a while, Chantal would come back to Beirut and ask me to read her a few verses of Baudelaire in my little studio at the front line. In my arms she would shoot up, weep, curse, cry and drink. She would hastily fuck me and then light a cigarette in the manner of a French nouvelle vague film star. She told me she had become a junkie because one day, in Paris, she had met a young Algerian from the *banlieue*. In a discotheque, he had grabbed her hand. She told me she had been dancing with her girl-friends and ignoring him, and then he seized her hand in a tight grip and pulled her closer to him. No one had ever pulled her close like that, she said, and she had never experienced such force and confidence. Her sensitive father, as she referred to him, was always gentle, tiptoeing around her emotions, careful about her feelings, never imposing anything on her . . . He wasn't spineless, her father, she assured me; he was fierce in his business dealings, stern in public, exact and fair with his employees, and he was a good provider, but when it came to his daughter . . . I was untouchable, Chantal said, and he would melt at the sight of me. I grew up without opposition, totally laissez-faire. Then one late evening in a Parisian nightclub, a skinny, dark North African Arab grabbed my hand tight and looked me in the eye and I let go of everything. Malek, he called himself at first. Then he revealed that his real name was Idris. He loved me and insulted me. He called me *la pute chretienne*. He couldn't understand how there could be non-Muslim Arabs who spoke, read and wrote Arabic better than he did. He would say, *Tu n'es pas Arabe, tu n'es même pas musulmane*. He was illiterate, and had fought for everything in his life. He would preach to me about the superiority of Islam, but I knew Islamic history better than he did. My father, the Christian, read everything—our house was full of Arabic literature and Arabic poets. I had read everything too. Idris only knew rituals, fasting and prayers and hear-say—stories and mythologies. When I corrected him about his misconceptions, he would get mad . . . But the sex was amazing, it was raw and real. We started to shoot up and fuck in abandoned buildings until I got hooked. I was on heroin in no time and funding his addiction and mine . . . I would ask my father for money and spend it on us. We burned it all on spoons and needles. He slapped me when I couldn't get him what he wanted . . . and then one day he abruptly turned to prayer. He was praying five times a day. He wanted to change, he said. He met an older man who taught him about *Taqwa*.

Once, I was asleep in his home. He woke me up and asked me to come with him to an apartment down the street. He said there were important men in town, men he loved and wanted to honour. They were workers who had just arrived from the south of Algeria, from his mother's village. They were illiterate and looking for someone to read the Quran for them before prayers. They had asked him to read, but he was too embarrassed to confess that he couldn't. So he asked me to do it. I said: But I am a woman.

He cut my hair, dressed me in baggy clothes and called me Bilal. We went to the apartment. There were five old men sitting on the floor, drinking tea. I greeted them, and Idris introduced me as Bilal and told them I was a good reader. He said that we would sit outside, in the hallway, and read aloud to them. He said there was not enough space in the living room and that I needed to concentrate and that the acoustics in the hallway were more suitable for the reading.

One of the old men stood up to offer me his chair, but Idris insisted the hallway was best. The men were a bit suspicious, and they must have found it odd, but I moved quickly to the corridor and started to recite in a loud, singing voice, similar to those I had heard in the Eastern churches of my youth.

I read the sura they requested, I sang it with strength and beauty, and I heard the men's pious replies. When it was over, I walked to the door as if to smoke a cigarette. Once outside, I ran. I ran to the metro and disappeared from Idris' life forever. I came back to Beirut where Idris wouldn't dare to follow me.

Everyone loves Beirut and everyone is scared of Beirut, Chantal told me. But I misunderstood her, El-Marquis said. Now his face looked older and less celebratory.

I encouraged her to sexually experience anything and everyone, he continued. But I failed to see that it wasn't sexuality that was imprisoning her, that sexual defiance wasn't her problem. It was her identity. She was alienated by a deep resentment of her surroundings, yes. Arab and Muslim culture was a part of her, but she was estranged from it too, and then there was the isolation of the war . . . Once, before she left me in the little studio, she told me, We no longer belong here, we are mutants, and our only choice is to become even more mutant so that we eventually leave and disappear from this region. We are nothing now but the residue of a defeated, conquered past and we are stubbornly holding on to old creeds, a few archaic rituals and the facade of Western modernity. But fuck the Arabs, she said, contradicting herself. The more I fucked them, the more I surrendered my body to them, the more I resented them and the more they resented me. I hate them, I hate their cigarettes, I hate their jokes, their essentialist chauvinistic religion. I hate the way they want to fuck me and leave me. I hate the way they want to buy me everything even when they can't afford it . . . and I hate that they are always asking to marry me when they mean to fuck me, to convert me. I hate the way they admire me, and the way they hate me. I also hate my parents' obliviousness, their passivity, their surrender, and how they live in their past glories, as if they will rule this place forever, as if they are superior to everyone. And then she closed the door and left.

Dear Pavlov, one last drink, please, and then I will leave you. This is taking longer than I anticipated.

Six months ago, on a rainy Beirut winter's day, Chantal called me and asked me to meet her in the little room where we had reunited over the years. After all these years, she had kept the keys to the door. I raced to the studio under the falling bombs, jubilant to see her again. I rushed up the stairs and opened the door . . . I saw her body dangling from the ceiling. She had hanged herself in that room with the window, above the bed. I noticed her cigarettes and her glass of wine on the windowsill, still full. Her feet pointed to the book she had left open on the white sheets. For the rest of my days, I will never make sense of it.

And now, my dear man, I am sick. Sometimes I think that I deserve death by hanging myself. I am no longer sure if I have corrupted youth for my own entertainment or as an attempt to liberate this society from its clutches on our bodies. I guess I tried to liberate my students, but in the process I must have confused some of them . . . Nevertheless, I hold on to my beliefs and I am more convinced now than ever that this world should be undermined. I do not have the courage to hang myself, so I guess I must still love myself after all. Or maybe I still cling to the conviction that I did the right thing.

In any case, repentance will never be a choice for me, regard-less of the tragedies I may have caused. I believe that it is through vice alone that we can undermine this world—but with age, one realizes that Nature has perfected indifference and immorality. The world always defeats us. All we can do is mimic it, not undermine it. Or maybe we can refuse it, and convince ourselves that we are constructing or imagining an alternative, like your pious father did. But we in the Society, dear Pavlov, have no illusions, no aspirations to flatter some God. Bodily urges are part of our nature, and we should never think of resisting them. In any case, I am sick . . . My death is very near and if you agree to take your father's place and help us, here is what I would like to do. And have no fear, I will send two of our members to facilitate things.

Pavlov again nodded silently.

Dear Pavlov, I am very happy that you agree. We will now consider you part of our society.

These are my wishes: I would like my body to be dressed in a woman's gown, a long gown that falls below my feet, and for my body to be hanged in the middle of my house. High up, near the ceiling. After my death, the house shall witness one last grand gathering and debauchery. Great acts of licen-tiousness shall take place without the knowledge or permis-sion of the authorities. But, most importantly, I want my body to hang there while Society members enjoy lavish food and drink, and then dance beneath me and have free and wild encounters—nothing is off-limits. At the end of the party, your role is to complete my wish: I wish to be burned to ashes, placed in a sealed plastic bag, not an urn, and for my dust to be given to Florence. She has agreed to take my remains to Paris on a tour of my favourite cemeteries—Père Lachaise, Montparnasse, Montmartre—and to sprinkle me on the graves of my favourite poets, with a larger portion on Oscar Wilde's and Rimbaud's graves. Did I mention that we will pay you handsomely? Of course, Florence's fat businessman husband does not know of our plan. As a matter of fact, I suggested that she drop a pinch of me in his food, which might cause him either a little indigestion or a good deal of enlightenment, and either case will be fine by me. And now, my dear man, since you have so kindly agreed, I will leave you to attend to your own matters.

Thank you in advance. My two associates, Hanneh and Manneh, will be in touch concerning various logistics and arrangements.

With this, El-Marquis turned to leave, then turned back.

And, oh yes—occasionally, members of the Society or an acquaintance might get in touch with you, dear Pavlov. I'll refer them to you and you will be paid accordingly. I hope you will enjoy my farewell party. I've chosen a truly fantastic dress for the event. I've already tried it, and it fits like a glove.

ANTIQUE DEALER

Pavlov called the local antique dealer and asked him to pay a visit to the family home. The dealer, who was French, was the husband of a neighbourhood woman named, not surprisingly, Marie (popular in this ancient Christian enclave). Marie had years ago befriended Pavlov's mother, Josephine, and had regularly visited when Josephine was alive to covertly assess the latest acquisitions from dead loners. In short, Marie was one of those few people who visited the undertakers. Josephine would scrub the floor on her two knees, her palms parallel, before Marie came over. This meek behaviour of his mother in front of a snooty lady married to a Frenchman who claimed to have lived in Nice and Paris made Pavlov sick.

He recalled how, when he was a kid, his mother would send him to get Marie the brand of cigarettes she preferred. Josephine would then offer Marie cigarettes and coffee, and sweets that she produced from nowhere. These sweets were hidden from the kids, covered in sugar, and in Pavlov's eyes, coated in treachery and repulsion. Marie, round-ankled Marie, would take one, moaning, *Que c'est bon Josephine, t'a fait toi même?* His mother would display all the china that his father had collected from the dead, parade the loot of the cadavers and lay it on the table, on the chair, stretching it towards the watchful ceiling.

Pavlov knew that the Frenchman, Monsieur Daniel, dealt in all kinds of lost and found, including stolen war loot. When Pavlov telephoned, the antique dealer rushed over, pushing through a procession for a dead child who was being drawn down the street in a small white coffin. As Pavlov stood at his window, watching the agony of the trail of mourners, he spotted the dealer. The Frenchman looked frantic, both apologetic and insincere as he crossed through the middle of the crowd, oblivious to the weeping, the beating of chests, the mother's sorrow and tears. Pavlov saw him sweep a hand across his mouth in anticipation, walking in haste, aiming straight for the entrance to Pavlov's home. In no time, he was knocking at the door. Pavlov did not bother to change his clothes and comb his hair. Monsieur Daniel was an arriviste, an opportunistic parasite who for many years had tried to buy the unclaimed possessions of the dead from Pavlov's father. But his father had always refused to sell the relics of the dead for fear they might reclaim them in his dreams.

Upon entering, the dealer asked Pavlov about a small Persian carpet that his mother, Josephine, had used to beat and dust every fall up on the roof. He confessed to Pavlov that during the carpet-slapping season, his love for good carpets made him take to the roofs and watch the beauty of every carpet's pattern, every lotus and branch exhaling soil, and every peacock figure coughing up the winter's filth carried by the shoes on all the visitors to a big house like Pavlov's. He claimed to have a record of every tapestry and rug that existed in the neighbourhood, in the hope that one day the legacy of every carpet would be honoured for eternity. But the possessive people of this land are attached to their carpets, Monsieur Daniel said, and they will keep them in their families for generations, until the very last one dies. Only death will free these carpets from their oppressors. Carpets move, travel, fly and migrate . . . but after the parents die, the dealer said, almost in tears, the children of the deceased would rather cut up the carpet and divide it into pieces out of spite during their disagreements over their inheritance. They prefer to each take a cut piece home than to sell it whole to a connoisseur, a lover of art. This happened once! I followed an intact carpet that I loved from one house to another, and I would visit its owner, pretending to be a friend of the family, or a man from outside with news from a distant cousin, just to have the pleasure of a walk upon it. I would even insist on taking off my shoes, even though nobody does that in this neighbourhood! Just so my toes could feel the exquisite stitching. Once, I even faked a heart attack to be closer to the carpet and lay my face on it! To sniff it and brush my cheeks against its threads of magnificent wool.

But I digress. Do you have anything that you want to sell, monsieur? I buy vases, certainly carpets, gold and silver ancient Phoenician tear cups, Roman busts, Greek vases, Mongols' archery bows, Islamic manuscripts, Syrian monks' translations of Aristotle's work from Syriac to Arabic, monks' filthy robes, Byzantine mosaics, golden crosses and communion cups silver or gold, precious stones, jewellery, crusaders' relics. The richness and historical layers of this city are its wealth and downfall. Let me help you liberate your people! Get rid of it all, all these artifacts that contribute to and justify tribal and religious affiliations! All these relics are an emblem of past disputes and contested land. Hand them to an expert outsider and watch how peace will prevail! Bombs shall cease and flowers shall bloom once all these historical artifacts are sold and shipped to France, *la Republique*! History is a curse, *mon ami*. My clients love to acquire all these objects and please, do not be fooled, we are not just merchants here, we take what has been buried and we reveal its beauty to the world. *Le partage*, monsieur! *Le partage universel.*

Pavlov escorted Monsieur Daniel into his parents' bedroom and the dealer half-fainted onto the bed. He rolled his eyes, then rolled himself onto the floor, touching everything and anything he could lay his fingers upon. He offered Pavlov a large sum of money to be free of it all.

Pavlov agreed on the amount. On one condition, he said.

I am listening, the dealer said.

I want your wife, Marie, to come over with the payment, a pack of my favourite cigarettes and a tray of coffee in her hand.

Bewildered, the Frenchman acquiesced. I will send her in the company of my son.

No, Pavlov objected. I want her to come alone.

C'est impossible! She is the same age as your mother, said Monsieur Daniel.

But Pavlov stood his ground until the Frenchman puffed and gesticulated, and then agreed to send his wife over with an amount that would sustain Pavlov's ascetic existence for many years to come.

And I will come back at night with my two sons to pack it all up, monsieur. As I said, my buyers hail from all over the world . . . You should be proud! he said, and chuckled. This country, this universe, will be a happier place. I believe in sharing . . . in heritage, the Frenchman declared as he glided towards the door, smelling of old objects with a hint of rust and mould.

L'heritage appartient à nous tous, he shouted up the stairs as he grabbed an Ottoman vase and made his way out.

That afternoon, Pavlov stood on his balcony and watched Madame Daniel making her way through the mud of the cemetery road with a tray in hand, a pot of coffee and two small cups. The chain of her handbag had slipped from her shoulder and swung from her hand. It must be the burden of the many cigarettes inside it, Pavlov thought.

Marie knocked, and climbed the stairs. Pavlov opened the door and instructed her to put the coffee on the table. He asked for the cigarettes, and she pulled her purse back onto her shoulder, opened it and slammed the pack down. Then she withdrew a large amount of money, handed it to him and said, The rest my husband and sons will bring tonight. I never liked you, Pavlov. Your mother would be ashamed of the way you treat her friends.

Pavlov, undeterred, asked her to howl like a dog if she and her husband wished to seal the deal. Marie obliged with two short, feeble barks and ran back down the stairs.

Pavlov walked to the window, faced his father's grave and proclaimed: I have sold it all. The dead won't be needing carpets to walk on, nice landscape paintings to imagine strolling in woods and across prairies, vases to revive cut flowers in, clothes to display on their decomposed bodies.

~

At midnight, there was a knock at Pavlov's door. It was the antique dealer and his two sons. The shorter rounder son was holding a candle and his shadow was not thin—it covered the stairwell behind him with the bleak totality of an astronomical eclipse.

Monsieur, the Frenchman whispered, we have to move in the dark and transport everything quickly. You know how people interfere and inquire in this neighbourhood. They have long noses and are always suspicious . . .

He and his sons tiptoed through Pavlov's home and quietly carried everything away, the thinner elder son, perhaps resentful about his mother's treatment, eyeing Pavlov with disgust.

But Monsieur Daniel seemed entirely happy, enthusiastic even, and before leaving he offered Pavlov a bottle of wine that he claimed to have found on one of his trips to the ruins of Baalbek.

It is a thousand years old, but I want you to have it. Because soon we are returning to France . . . And as much as we would like to carry it, wine is hard to transport. Some of our goods, he said čandidly, will cross the Syrian border. We know people we can trust. Then we shall fly the stock to Corsica and finally Europe. Collectors and museums shall acquire them, date them, catalogue them, dust them off and eventually display them. One day you should come to France. We will give you the tour, *le tour de France*! he said and his fat younger son laughed quietly and pedalled his hands, one leg up in the air.

A family joke, the dealer said. Monsieur, *je suis le sauveur des valeurs humaines et vous aussi*, he added.

The younger son placed his hand on Pavlov's shoulder and repeated, *Et vous aussi*.

Yes, Pavlov said. Now hurry up and take it all. And do not forget the shoes and the clothes.

The dealer bowed his head. Yes, we will go now and enjoy these splendid *oeuvres* I have acquired from all the beautiful houses here. As for *l'heritage*, consider this my gift to humanity!

Au revoir, the Frenchman said, and his two sons repeated his words, *Au revoir, au revoir*.

THE DEATH OF TARIQ
THE DOG OWNER

Pavlov extended his ears to listen to a group of men who were standing under his balcony. They were talking about a local young fighter by the name of Tariq who would soon be buried. This fighter, at the age of seventeen, had joined the militia and, after a battle in a once-fancy hotel downtown that lasted two days, he and five of his friends, having run out of ammunition, threw themselves from the twenty-fourth floor. Their enemies had managed to surround them from the upper and the lower floors. The men on Pavlov's street claimed that, in fact, the fighters were captured and thrown from the window of the hotel.

But Pavlov was convinced that Tariq had jumped of his own will. Tariq owned a dog named Rex, and Pavlov used to watch him from the window walking his dog every morning. The dog was fond of bones and graves, and often squeezed between the bars of the locked gate and ran inside the cemetery. Pavlov had often seen the young fighter climb over the stone wall to chase the dog out, and then climb back onto the wall and jump with a sublime drop, arms stretched out, eyes open, hair flowing above his head, until the soles of his shoes landed on firm grass, his knees bent and head held upright with pride and dignity. Oh, how fearless and good-looking, Pavlov had thought. He and I are lovers of heights and admirers of gravity.

Standing now in his kitchen, Pavlov knew he would soon hear the drumbeat of the brass band—the singular, repeating beat usually executed by an eager band member. This band was only ever invited to play music for the youthful dead. And upon hearing it, Pavlov would salivate and feel the urge to shift his hips and stretch his back before padding out to the balcony.

He hurried to buy cigarettes before the horizontal passage of the dead, putting on his dark suit and rushing out to the end of the street to catch the grocer before the man lowered his metal door. He was determined to get his pack of cigarettes and his favourite brand of matches. Through the years, he had learned the value of fire and wood. Hindus, unlike the Abrahamic sons of this region, burn their dead—this he had learned from his father the undertaker—as did the Greeks of antiquity. And it was the duty, his father had said, of the male heir to light the fire. The idea of a grand bonfire in place of a coffin intrigued Pavlov. He imagined himself standing on his balcony and watching the flickering light, little floating red particles, his ceremonial cigarette joining the fleeting *étincelles* as his own contribution to the burning. Earth and the ground are overrated, his father had said. It is smoke that matters, that fleeing gesture of escape that reaches beyond lands and borders and claimed territories. He remembered his father speaking of the universality of fire, the antiquity of the flame, and quoting Heraclitus: All things change to fire, and fire, exhausted, falls back into all things.

Poor terrestrial dead, Pavlov thought, miserable cadavers confined to their rectangular demarcation. They have to endure the crushing weight of the earth, and the bird's-eye view of apathetic gravediggers pouring earth into their eyes. He hurried back home, lit a cigarette and stood on his balcony. He inhaled and exhaled with force, and bade farewell to the smoke on this day of light rain and blossoming trees and the shameless appearance of flowers, pink pirouettes exuberant with scent and colour that mingled with bullets falling from weapons in the hands of fighters wearing cheap white sneakers with green rubber soles made in China.

And now the brass band played, and the mourners arrived. When the dead was a young, unmarried man like Tariq, the custom was to dance with the coffin, enacting the missed and now impossible wedding, while carrying it down the burial road. But how had this custom of dancing coffins, which Pavlov had simply accepted all these years, come about? He suddenly thought, What an absurd idea—to dance with wooden boxes carrying a dead person inside. What a parade, a charade, a mockery of the fine art of dancing . . . Oh, the nausea of death, he thought, the vomit of the stiff on padded silk pillows. The rattling of devils' tails inside the red entrails of a satin coffin, and the smell of powdered baby angels, must have made the corpse quite dizzy.

As a kid, when his father had stood solemnly at the cemetery gate awaiting the approach of a dancing casket, Pavlov would stand on this same balcony and laugh, dancing to the music of the marching band. The six men lifting the box created the shape of a wobbly, mythical creature with twelve arms, twelve legs swaying its way towards the edge of a manmade pit. The band played tunes for which Pavlov made up various names: The Dance of Drunken Coffins, A Weeping of Happy Feet, An Enchanting Choice of Radio Music. And he would wonder about the positions of the grooms inside the boxes on their bumpy ride towards the grand altar down below.

Then one day his mother had smacked him hard on the head and called him blasphemous. What if the parents of the dead see you? You're not supposed to do this. Who taught you to laugh? All those books you've been reading, have they made you insensitive and corrupt! To punish him, she threatened to burn his books, especially those of the Greeks he so often quoted in his youth.

Now Pavlov watched with a tiny smile and wondered again: Who had started this daring custom of dancing with coffins? It couldn't have been the Egyptians, he reasoned, because pharaohs were married at a very early age, and even from the little reading he had done on Egyptian ritual, Pavlov had concluded they were not as crass about their burials as his own bastard nation of invading Canaanites, Egyptians, Hittites, Persians, Greeks, Romans, Vikings, Arabs, Mongols, crusaders, pirates and Turks. Imagine, he thought, if every once in a while a young cadaver were to leave his coffin and chase a few nearby virgins or widows to try to consummate his marriage. Yes, he reasoned, weddings and burials are the same. Exactly the same. In both, weeping and celebration exist side by side. They are part of the dialectic that includes hermaphrodites and semi-gods, the Manichaean stripes of zebras, double agents in war movies, Siamese twins, divided cities, border rivers and Homeric sirens of the sea.

On this day of Tariq the fighter's burial, mourners danced and wept, and the deceased's dog trailed the pack of men to the cemetery. There, the dog stopped at the gate and whimpered and howled, then walked to the foot of the wall, sniffing in search of his master. The dog lay there all night.

In the morning, before dawn, Pavlov brought Rex some water, a handful of cooked rice and vegetables, and small pieces of meat.

OF UNCLES AND COUSINS

Pavlov's twin uncles, Maurice (the elder) and Mounir (the younger)—or the two big sweaty brutes, as Pavlov called them—lived at the edge of the cemetery in a three-storey house with their funeral home on the ground floor. The elder resided on the third floor, with his wife; and the younger on the second floor with his wife, their ever-laughing daughter Salwa and their idiotic son Pierre.

The business had been started by Pavlov's father, who later hired his brothers and helped build their two homes above the funeral parlour. The ground-floor business had a showroom in front and a large vault at the back where the caskets were kept. This was also where blood was drained and bodies cleaned, stitched, dressed up and made up. In these years of war, business was booming.

After the death of his father, Pavlov and his sister had sold their father's share of the enterprise to their uncles. The uncles took full possession of the ground floor, including the leftover coffins, the tools, the disinfecting chemicals and the chrome tables, and two of the hearses—or "deathmobiles" as Pavlov termed them. The twins had paid Pavlov and Nathalie a small advance, and promised to pay the rest soon after. His sister asked Pavlov to hold one of the hearses as collateral for the payment.

Pavlov detested his uncles. They were so different from his father, these twin brutes, these vultures who—in the absence of their brother—now walked the grounds of the cemetery at night, opening newly buried coffins to collect rings, shoes, crucifixes, cufflinks, necklaces, memorabilia, even flowers, if still fresh, to reuse at the next burial. From his window, he could see their flashlights whirling, like confused nocturnal creatures. He heard their laughter and deadpan jokes. In their quiet, mocking voices, they would address the cadavers using villagers' accents: O So-and-so, hear me now and may the devil have mercy on your soul, and allow me to hold your hand and check the time on your expensive wristwatch. I hear that these leather shoes are too tight on you . . . I will stretch them a bit while you're busy dancing with the devil's wife there . . .

These brutes sometimes even brought along the younger's dimwitted son and daughter with her hyena laugh. Once in a while, when delinquent kids tried to sneak into the cemetery at night to spray-paint tombs with war slogans, making their mark on destiny with their heroic lettering and fighters' nicknames, the younger brute would send Salwa out alone, to release her hyena laugh. She would laugh even louder when the kids fled, throwing themselves over the fences and pissing their pants, trembling in horror and fear.

One afternoon, these twin uncles Maurice and Mounir knocked at Pavlov's door and asked for the second hearse. With the torrent of war deaths, they needed the extra car. Pavlov refused—unless they first paid the balance owed to him and his sister. The uncles promised to pay it soon, but Pavlov still would not give them the key or the registration papers. Maurice, the elder, told him that his father was watching from above and would be ashamed of his behaviour and his greed. Pavlov slammed the door shut, then opened it to warn his uncles not to touch the car or come to the house again without bringing what they owed. Mounir, the hotheaded younger uncle, threatened Pavlov—but Pavlov laughed at him. Then he barked and bared his teeth, and the uncles slunk away.

JEAN YACOUB

A stranger knocked at Pavlov's door.

My name is Jean Yacoub, the man said. I was referred to you by the Society. May I come in?

Pavlov ushered him inside.

You must be Pavlov, the man said.

Pavlov nodded and offered him cigarettes and coffee.

The man accepted a cigarette but didn't touch the coffee. He seemed reluctant to speak, murmuring platitudes about the tailbacks he had encountered on his way through town. A big sinkhole had caused masses of traffic, he said.

Finally, Pavlov quietly, gently asked him the purpose of his visit.

Well, the man said, hesitantly. Then he spoke in a rush, without pause: My wife left me and ran away to France with another man. Now she is remarried and has her own life and family there. I used to lock her inside our house, demanding that she read a book a day, and telling her that when I got back from work I would test her. I did this to make sure that she never left the house for long or cheated on me. But later I found out that she didn't read the books and made up the stories she told me. She knew I hadn't read the books either. Eventually she left, got married again and had children, leaving me with our son. She put our marriage behind her.

My great tragedy is the loss of my son. Years ago, I discovered that my son had a preference for men . . . You know what I mean. To put it bluntly, he was homosexual. When I found out, I disowned him. He left the house and never came back. Two years passed and I never asked anyone of his whereabouts. Still, I heard that he was living with a lover, a man. So I knew he was having sex with men, and at the time the thought of this repulsed me. I couldn't deal with the idea of it, the profanity, the filth involved, these acts of sodomy that I imagined. It haunted me. I even sent him a message through his aunt, who was accepting of his condition, reiterating that I had disowned him.

After the war broke out, on one of those nights of bombardment, my son showed up at my door, drunk, in the company of a militia thug—his lover, I assumed. The man was in uniform, with a gun at his waist and a large golden cross on his chest. I remember he had a bear's build and a killer's eyes. He and my son sat facing me on the sofa. In my house, they chain-smoked and played with each other's hair and kissed. All this was meant to provoke me. When I objected and told them to leave, my son's lover pulled out the gun and laid it on the coffee table in front of my eyes. He then picked up the gun, waved it in my face and said that if I ever tried to contact my son again, he would kill me. Imagine. And my son laughed. He didn't mind seeing me humiliated by this hooligan, this piece of excrement who threatened his father in his own home.

A few months later, my sister, who by then had invited my son to live with her, knocked at my door wailing and screaming. She informed me that my son had been shot and killed on the stairs of her building.

I was devastated. Death makes one forgive and love again. We humans only value our losses and regrets. I am a despicable man, Mr. Pavlov. My son is extinct. My sister has since died. She couldn't take the loss—maybe because she loved my son more than I did. She felt responsible, and she died from sadness. I am now alone.

When my son was shot, I was told, he was high and making love to another man on the stairs of my sister's building. He had been spotted by a warlord who was coming down from his apartment with two of his men. They shot my son and his lover on the spot. Then they stuck the bodies in a jeep, drove to the beach and threw them into a dumpster. No one claimed the bodies. And no one knew my son's whereabouts. This story is true. I heard later that the warlord's bodyguards bragged about killing two homosexuals.

I tried to find my son's body, in vain. I wanted to cry over his body that had caused both of us so much pain. And I wanted to properly mourn him.

For years, I asked every hospital in Beirut about my son's remains, but could find no answer. I tried to complain to the militia, but they gave me the runaround. They even sent two men to threaten me. I started to pray again. I prayed for forgiveness from a God who never forgave my son, a God who had refused him the freedom to live as he desired, a God who taught me to refuse my son's desires. But one day, I found I was tired of blaming myself. When I thought about it, I realized I had blamed everything on that God, the same God I had asked forgiveness from. It is confusing, isn't it, dear Pavlov? To demand forgiveness from your oppressors.

I became obsessed with men who have effeminate mannerisms. I would walk around my neighbourhood and observe them with a mixture of pity, sadness and love. That is when I encountered El-Marquis in the elevator of my building. I introduced myself and asked if I might have a private conversation with him. He smiled and said, And what is on your mind?

My son who died, I said. He preferred the company of men.

El-Marquis ignored the fact that the elevator had arrived at his floor and continued on with me. At my invitation, he entered my home.

We sat. He asked for a drink. Then he said, Many parents consider the act of love between two men degenerate.

I did, I said. But I no longer think so. My loss was devastating. Morality looks banal in the presence of such a grand and total loss.

El-Marquis nodded and gave me your father's name. And he told me about his work picking up unclaimed cadavers, and about his love of fire.

The next day, I walked to the cemetery across the road from your house. I observed your father standing at the gate, murmuring his own prayers and carrying a small torch in his hand. He looked different—concerned, and not blasé, like one would expect an undertaker to be. The next day, I visited him on the pretext of arranging my own funeral. The first thing I said to him was, Fire is better than dust. And his face lit up.

After he had heard my story, he told me that two springs earlier he had recovered two male bodies from the Quarantina garbage dump by the shore. These bodies had been beaten, and their sex had been shot. One of them was wearing women's underwear and had straight hair and a small diamond in his ear. He showed me the diamond.

I knew straight away that these were the bodies of my son and his friend.

Your father confessed to me that he had secretly cremated them and performed his own prayers, against the dictates of the clergy in this land, and spread their ashes in a valley up in the mountains. He said that he would eventually take me there but the location had to remain a secret because he lived in fear of the clergy's wrath.

I was very ill and in hospital for a while after that. So my trip with your father had to be postponed. And then, a little while ago, I learned that he had died.

When we were talking, your father also mentioned you, his son. He said "we," and he said your name. Were you present when your father scattered my son's ashes? You are now my only link, my only hope to rectify the wrongs I have done in my life.

I am a dying man and I am asking you to do the same thing for me that your father did for my poor son. After my death, I ask you to burn me and spread my ashes in the same valley as my son and his lover. I will pay you handsomely, and I will also arrange to have my body delivered to you. I am alone. Everyone around me has fled or died. No one will notice my absence. I have no one and nothing left but my wish to take last flight in the same place as my son.

The man stopped speaking, and looked at Pavlov.

I can help you, Pavlov said.

The man withdrew some cash and set it on the table.

The rest of the money will be delivered with my body, he said. Thank you.

And with this, Jean Yacoub stood and left.

INTRODUCING THE
LADY OF THE STAIRS

In a peaceful moment—when bombs were not falling so close as to obscure the rosy, sunny morning that was about to imbue the old trees in the cemetery with shades of green, when the sand in the shape of immobile dunes was dispersed by the morning air to expose a crust of the soil above the skeleton of the earth, when the headstones weighted by the corpulence of years were cloaked with resilient layers of bright moss—here was Pavlov, standing at his window. He was watching a procession slowly moving towards the gate, a warm cup of coffee in his hand, its steam ascending to block the rays of the sun, when he heard the swift whistle of a bomb preparing to land on the road below his window. Glass shattered and fell on Pavlov's head, and he saw a cloud of grey, dense smoke, and then he sensed a ponderous silence in his chest. In that silence, he heard a faint moan creeping up from below. He stood and walked out onto his balcony and glanced at the road.

There was a casket on the ground. It was surrounded by injured and dead mourners, their bodies in black, lying flat, parallel to the earth. Heads, thighs, shoes, blood. Death was everywhere. Burials will be required, Pavlov murmured. A bomb had landed in front of the priest and shredded him. The body was lying on the ground without a head, decapitated. The priest's shoe, filled with his five toes and an ankle, had landed on Pavlov's balcony.

Pavlov ran down the stairs to the street. Frantic, panting, and with a piece of glass piercing his forehead, he rushed to help the injured, piling them into cars heading to the hospitals. His uncles, who had been awaiting the casket at the cemetery gate, stood unmoving, eyes wide in amazement, taking in their good fortune. Salwa, Pavlov's cousin, started to release her loud nocturnal laugh while her brother Pierre went home to call his mother and aunt to attend the spectacle.

A young woman wandering aimlessly in shock came to rest at the entrance to Pavlov's home. She sat on the ground, covered in blood. Pavlov offered his help, but she didn't seem injured. She had lost her entire family, she told him. She screamed then laughed and mumbled, and then she lost her mind. They're coming, coffee no sugar, coffee no sugar, she repeated. They just went there . . . They are coming back, they are here, welcome . . . Make coffee, bring chairs . . . Pavlov took her by the hand and led her just inside, to the bottom stair. He looked into her vacant eyes and realized that she had gone mad. So he left her with her incantations of hospitality and rushed outside once more to attend to the injured.

Howling and incoherent screams and shouts filled the dusty road in vertical and horizontal trajectories that disoriented him. In the chaos of blood and wounded limbs, everything seemed oddly palpable. Everything had either ceased to move or moved in slow motion, as flashing images and low voices alternating with screams reached his ears. He stood in the middle of a canvas of fragmented bodies arranged in a careful geometrical shape with a rectangular coffin at the centre, a coffin that had split in half, the lid resting a few metres away on the side of the dirt road. And among all the wounded and the dead, it seemed that the body in the coffin was the only one that had managed, willingly or miraculously, to remain intact—except for a pair of shoes that had been blown off, exposing the cadaver's toes. The procession had disintegrated. No one stood upright, and everything lay flat like paper. The end of *Homo erectus*, thought Pavlov. The straight sombre line of mourners had been torn to pieces—or, at best, the mourners were on the ground, some crawling and exclaiming their thirst, others burned and choking with smoke and blood. There was no music, no orderly walking, no priest showing the path towards eternity. All that existed was killing and death, and from that moment on, Pavlov, who had all his life witnessed burials on this road but never mass murder, realized that the ceremonies that passed under his window had no meaning, that randomness was everything, and that from early childhood he had been a spectator to life's cruelest acts of extinction.

Now more cars rushed towards the cemetery road to pick up the wounded, and again a crescendo of shouts, an uproar, a pandemonium of agonizing howls rose and remained suspended in the air, the echo of wounds and death, red gushing from unbolted skin, moans of the dying and then the dignifying silence of those considerate victims, the ones who listen but do not speak, who weigh their words before exhaling their last breath, fixing their open eyes on one direction, one single image that asserts the void of life. Pavlov was left with a sharp pain in his head, beside a coffin that lay in perfect stillness in the middle of the dirt road. With blood pouring down his face, he stumbled, stepped on a body and fell beside it. The piece of glass seemed to penetrate farther into his head. Then he heard a crack inside his skull and saw the small fragment falling from his forehead to the ground, where the sun struck it and a feeble ray shone into his eyes. And he too started to scream as he got up and rushed towards an injured woman, blood dripping over his eyes, nose, chin. With his white shirt soaked, his red face and newly cardinal-like attire, he frightened the woman he was seeking to assist. He tried frantically to help her up, but she resisted and screamed hysterically. Other survivors were screaming also, calling out people's names, walking as if dazed by smoke following a eucalyptus fire. The unholy smell of powder, metal and flesh joined that of holy incense around the coffin. Stray shoes were scattered across the ground. Some mourners died with their faces towards the earth while others faced the clouds, the blue of the sky reflected in their eyes, two bright dots in a sea of red.

By now, Pavlov's uncles were carrying cadavers from the centre of the road and laying them at the curb, arranging them by height and the size of their feet. Salwa was standing still, her laughter quieter, turning into chuckles. Then once again she released her disturbing cackle, which to Pavlov's ears shifted between pure wickedness and a philosophical cry that summarized the absurdity of the world. Pavlov walked over to Salwa and slapped her hard. Her head swung to the left, bounced back, and she laughed once more in a short, loud burst. Then she fell silent and walked away without uttering a sound.

Back home, drenched in blood and sorrow, Pavlov found the woman who had lost her entire family sitting on his stairs. She refused to come with him upstairs. He pulled her hand, but she held on to the rail and moaned in protest. Her brother and mother had died in the bomb, and so had her uncle and four of her relatives, and now she refused to leave the stairs. Finally, Pavlov walked up to his home, made coffee, and went back down with a tray in his hand and a glass of water. The woman started to cry again. She refused his offerings of coffee or food or liquid of any sort. Frustrated, he rushed back upstairs, splashed his face with water, wrapped his own bleeding head, drank water and sunk his head low in the basin of the sink. He started to whimper and mumble, until gradually every sound turned into an incomprehensible language in front of the cruelty of the mirror and the dismal abyss of the sink.

Eventually he went downstairs again and looked closely at the woman. He realized that he knew who she was. He remembered her father's burial two years ago and recalled the simplicity of the ceremony. He also remembered how she had held a delicate white lace handkerchief as she walked in the procession below his window. She had been modest in her pain, her arms around her little brother's shoulders. She had wept that day, embracing her brother all the way, but today it was Pavlov who had carried her brother's body to the back seat of a car. He had thrown the boy into the vehicle with complete disregard for his lightness and the possibility that he might take flight. It must have been his nerves, Pavlov decided, and his eagerness to run back to the others who were injured, that had made him throw the boy with such velocity. The body, in Pavlov's memory, had hovered for a fraction of a second. This image of the boy above the car seat, suspended before the fall, hesitant even in death, stayed on Pavlov's mind—a body that had the power to extend its position before landing, he thought, as if drawing a last breath, gathering a last burst of energy, one that all creatures express before annihilation, the last kick of prey pursued by predator, the last word, the last dance, a sigh. And then there are those who are fortunate enough to have the last laugh at this cruel existence.

Yes, this woman's little brother, who had walked wrapped in her arms during their father's funeral procession, had been swinging in Pavlov's arms today—or was it yesterday? His head hurt, and for once he felt himself to be an imposter who had stumbled upon a grand spectacle and forced his way in, a man who had left his seat in the audience and walked up on stage, interrupting a play, to the jeers of the spectators and the annoyance of the actors. Or was he more like a madman who, manifesto in hand, manages to release a few condemning words at the podium before being pounced upon and muffled by guards, and treated not as a rebel but as a fool . . .

He sat down next to the woman on the stairs. Surely she must have been hit by shrapnel from the bomb, or pierced by glass, or even cut by flying pebbles or the body parts of the injured—a flapping lip, or sharp, high cheekbones, a wandering eye. He made the woman stand up and inspected her dress for blood, patted her back and hair, but she seemed intact, incredibly intact: all the blood and dirt attached to her had its genesis elsewhere. She again refused to go up the stairs with him. Pavlov sighed, lit a candle and began to pick small, dry blood clots from her hair. She let him do this—she even laughed and smiled at him—and then she slept.

The next day, he brought her water and food. He fetched warm water in a large bucket, and calmly and affectionately asked her to take off her clothes, and washed her from head to toe at the bottom of the stairs. She clutched her arms around herself and rocked against the railing, playing with her own hair and laughing occasionally, a sound somewhere between a snigger and a belly laugh.

This is farcical, Pavlov thought, it's all a farce, and he laughed along with her.

That night, he dreamed of coffins marching along the street. He saw himself standing at the window, watching a large figure in a long white robe swinging a stick while swaying and dancing against the tide of the procession and sweeping a cane in the air. Those it touched perished, and those it missed lived to regret not being touched by it. A dance, Pavlov imagined. A dance performed by death itself.

Death continued to silently sway after the instruments fell to the ground and the music ceased. The figure in the white robe came and went, then disappeared into the horizon between outstretched bodies and headstones.

It's all just a dance, Pavlov thought. And nothing is more devastating than a dance.

In April, the streets and the dust turned wet. The last rains fell in the company of bombs and bullets, transforming the sky into sustained, menacing thunder. Beirut, the grey city with its few remaining faint-yellow houses and its uneven pavement and its incoherent, convoluted roads, was humbled by the rain and the little streams rushing towards the French stairs that stretched from the top of the Achrafieh hills towards the lower city before reaching the port and the Mediterranean Sea.

Ever since the massacre below Pavlov's balcony, the city had been preoccupied with the seriousness of war and oblivious to its own ancient rain. The dancing for the dead had stopped, and so too had the long, slow marches towards the graveyard. Now people buried their dead in haste. They looked up anxiously for signs of destruction and listened for the bombs' whistles. Families avoided the burial road; now only men walked in the dusty procession. Kids and women still spent their nights in vigils beside corpses, as was the custom, but now they bade farewell at their doorsteps, wailing and throwing themselves on the coffins in the manner of ancient Achaeans. Their crying and weeping no longer took place below the window of the man who affiliated himself with dogs.

Soon, a new type of burial replaced the old. Young fighters stopped in front of Pavlov's house in their military cars, wanting to bury their brothers in arms. The few musicians in the band who had survived the massacre were replaced by militia indifferent to scales and notes. Now, at the passage of their fallen comrades, these fighters raised their guns in the air and shot towards the clouds.

GUNSHOT

One afternoon, as a crescendo of bells on one side of the city asserted the call to prayer, and the pleas of the muezzins on the other side called for submission to God, Pavlov stood at his newly repaired window. He was watching a platoon of Christian militiamen facing his balcony. They stood in a row with their rifles raised towards the sky, ready to pay respects to a fallen comrade. One of the men looked at Pavlov and angled his rifle towards his window. At a signal from the head of the platoon, the militiamen fired. The bullet from the fighter who aimed at Pavlov missed by a couple of centimetres. It hit the wall and a small poof rose from the yellow-painted stone. Dust and particles fell on the road below.

The young man had aimed to kill. Pavlov was sure of it. This warrior's fire was not a mistake, a joke, or a protest at Pavlov's voyeuristic position high above. The fighter had the look of murder—clear intent, index finger curved on the rifle's trigger, and lunatic eyes that flashed in Pavlov's mind with the same brightness as a gun's barrel. He recalled the sharp, quick gesture of the fighter angling his rifle slightly, just enough to change the bullet's direction from a homage to a kill. No, not a protest, this was not a protest, Pavlov concluded. This was not an objection to Pavlov's fixed gaze, nor a statement of disrespect for the dead, nor anger at Pavlov's vista overlooking the military and their martyrs. This was an act of deliberate design: to kill a spectator.

And that spectator is me, Pavlov thought. Perhaps this was a banal killing for the sake of killing, just because this fighter could—in this time of lawlessness, in this age of carelessness and hate, in this civil war that opened windows of opportunity for the most impoverished, that elevated the deprived, the deranged, the meek with a yearning for vengeance and scores to settle. Yes, it was a time for the deprived to shine and take possession of the land; it was a time for the working men who once stood behind vegetable carts enduring petty negotiations and complaints about freshness to stand tall; it was a time of epiphany for the workers who had lugged their tool boxes up marble stairs to fix tubes and leaks in grand houses parading naked figures on expensive vases. Now these workers had discovered the benefits of gunshot. Now those sons of porters who had once run up and down stairs carrying groceries to the upper-class madame who couldn't be bothered to cover her transparent nightgown in the presence of the help, who never stopped giving orders and striding about with her bare feet on polished marble floors, saying, Leave the bag here and not there, and carry this downstairs, and tell

your coworkers to bring . . . this afternoon . . . and fix the—
upon which the husband would land a tip right in the middle
of the porter's palm, giving him resentment and ideas about
the value of revolutionary guns—now, in their military
fatigues, how proud they look, and how dangerous they are.

So why not fire at a man standing at a window above the
line of death and shotguns? After all, accidents were common
in the fertile presence of war. Pavlov had heard and seen it
all, passing under his balcony. He knew of a young man who
had shot another over a motorcycle ride. He knew of a fighter
who had stepped on a land mine and miraculously trotted to
safety—only to encounter another land mine. He knew of a
boy who had mistaken a grenade for a toy; a stray bullet from
a wedding celebration that had landed in someone's head;
traffic disputes that had resulted in deaths; villagers mistaken
for birds and killed by urban hunters; and other inexplicable
murders of passion, greed, machismo, idiocy, sexual bravado,
domestic violence . . . in addition to heart attacks and old age
and death multiplied a thousandfold.

Perhaps this attempt on his life was a warning. Pavlov
knew that his fixed gaze, his silent position, must make this
pious, militaristic community, where hierarchies and heights
were taken seriously, uneasy. But in fact, hardly anyone ever
looked up towards him during processions. Rather, the tra-
jectory of a mourner's gaze was almost always a sliding slope
towards the ground. Since childhood, he had stood at this same
window and watched, confident he was rarely noticed or seen.

It dawned on Pavlov that he was acquainted with the kid
who had shot at his window. He had known this kid's parents,

had watched their caskets passing under his window when his own father was still alive. The kid had changed since then; he had grown rougher. The kid's father had been a mechanic, a superstitious fool who had refused to admit Pavlov's father's hearse to the garage for repairs. The mechanic had feared cars that carried the dead. The kid who had shot at Pavlov used to help his own father in the garage, and would linger there, grabbing tires, rolling himself in an oval oil spot on the cement ground, his face covered in black smudges and engine grease as he moved with the slow momentum of lava flowing downhill.

Yes, Pavlov remembered this kid. Once, when Pavlov was young, he'd been sent by his father to the garage, with a message for the mechanic. He recalled seeing the kid who had just tried to kill him emerge, greasy, assisting his father with the tools. Pavlov had envied the son, had envied the pagan, primitive disguise that the oil from the machines bestowed on the kid's face, clothes and hands. Ah, he had thought, to walk like a heathen with a line of grease on your face, to camouflage yourself in bright daylight before everyone's eyes, to leave your finger marks on your own forehead, to be different in your attire, careless, marked, seen and unseen, revered and mocked, your sweat turning to liquid grey lines— the alchemy of it all, to be able to fix a machine in a chaos of grease, sweat and paint. It had hurt Pavlov back then to see the shame the kid felt as he worked away underneath the upraised cars. He looked away when he saw Pavlov, and tried to erase the stains on his skin with a pitiful grimy cloth. He had wiped his hands, Pavlov remembered, and tossed the cloth towards the tool box. Pavlov had imagined the cloth as travelling dark matter, suspended between the kid and the smudged wall before eventually, inescapably, landing gracefully on the metal counter.

But now a military uniform had wiped away all the grease, erased the sublime art of those grey traces. Perhaps the kid had joined the militia to remove the stain of his shame. War had provided him with a clean slate, a new beginning full of respect and order, opportunities. War had turned screws into bullets, snot into a moustache, stained sneakers into high boots, the evocative dirty calendar in his father's garage into real-life conquests. The car jack in the kid's hand had turned into an AK-47—it was still a mechanical object after all, and both cars and guns were complicit in modern-day death.

Pavlov wondered if the kid had tried to kill him out of shame over his earlier, stained self, or because Pavlov had once witnessed him being beaten. That day when Pavlov had visited the garage, the mechanic had beaten his son. He had pulled the kid's ear and spanked him hard, leaving big smudges on the kid's neck and buttocks. Perhaps this son of a mechanic blamed his father's brutish ways on undertakers and their kind—ghosts who reminded him of humiliation and death. Maybe Pavlov's presence at the window brought back memories of a father who had smeared grease on the doorknobs of the house with calloused, dirty hands that were bashed and bruised, with hammer-flattened nails. Perhaps the kid remembered the taste of grease in the family dinner, how engine lubricants had prevented domestic stability, how everything that had skidded and slid in the mechanic's home could be blamed on the undertakers who watched from above with an air of detachment, perhaps even superiority. Perhaps the slaps that the kid's father landed on his mother late at night, after smearing grease on clear bottles of booze and leaving the stains of his affection on the kid's face, could be conveniently blamed on the family of undertakers and its watchful descendant; after all, these same undertakers had delivered the last remains of the mechanic's life to the junk-yard of crosses and death.

To the young would-be assassin below, Pavlov knew, he must certainly have appeared like a ghost, an intrusive ghost from childhood, a mocking ghost who had witnessed the kid's shame, a ghost unafraid of the flight of a bullet and the possibility of death. That day, all this son of the mechanic had to do was tilt his gun a little, just a fraction of an angle, and fire towards the image at the window.

Now Pavlov smiled as he stood his ground. If the young man had killed him, no one would mourn, question or care. Pavlov's family of undertakers had never been held in high regard. And naturally, there was always humour in the death of an undertaker. The story of his own father's death—how his father's remains had fallen into the pit that he was dig-ging—had become a joke in the community. Everyone saw the irony and no one held back their mockery. They should have left him there and saved themselves the trouble, people said. If he had known, he would have brought a measuring tape, other malicious mortals said. Some burials are quick and done at a discount . . .

Pavlov looked the fighter in the eye and stood his ground.

Of the twenty-one ceremonial bullets that had been fired into the air, only one had gone in Pavlov's direction. Pavlov, in defiance, remained at the window, looking down at the fighters lifting their rifles and counting backwards as they fired once more. He had adopted the way of a dog and made a point of never showing fear or hesitation in moments of pain or danger.

The son of the mechanic could have adjusted his aim for a better shot. But the kid was indecisive about a second tilt of the gun. This was why Pavlov understood the shot to be a warning. After all, who would dare to kill a person who belonged to the race of earth-diggers, casket-makers, carpenters of doom, breeders of worms, depositors of bones, people who lived so intimately close to the dead with their hovering ghosts? Ghosts, Pavlov thought, could be scared, booed away, exorcised—but not killed and never fully buried. They hovered in the middle somewhere, suspended between two planes, and that was perhaps why the kid must have hesitated to aim once more towards the window and kill him.

Once, when Pavlov was a boy, his small soccer team had lost a game. After the match, as Pavlov was coming out of the bathroom, one of the other kids had come up to him and said that he should never have been allowed to join the team because he was a bad omen. This kid had pushed him to the ground and four other boys stomped on him and threw him against the edge of the pissing wall. One of them started to shout, Bury him! The others repeated, Bury him.

The son of the mechanic had been there. He stood nearby and watched silently, without participating—maybe because he was on the other team. Pavlov remembered opening his bloody mouth at the son of the mechanic, who ran away in horror, a grease stain on his shoes.

Now, after the militia had finished firing and carried their comrade's coffin to its grave, Pavlov stepped away from his window. He walked down the stairs and crossed to the cemetery gate. Inside the graveyard, he stood at the edge of the freshly dug pit and faced Son of Mechanic. And watched silently as this fighter, bewildered, struggled to hold back his tears.

SUMMER

THE PRIEST'S FRAGMENTS

One morning in late June, Pavlov, still in his pyjamas and slippers, rushed along the street to get his French Gitanes Maïs cigarettes before the grocery's metal doors, in deference to the impending passage of death, rolled down with the speed of a guillotine.

The grocer was sitting outside his store with a pack of men. Pavlov hurried inside, thinking the grocer would follow, but instead the fellow jumped up and locked the metal door on him, to the amusement of the men on the sidewalk. Pavlov was captive. He stood in darkness, confined to the company of vegetables, glass bottles of soda, packs of cigarettes and chocolates, and other familiar groceries: his favourite sweets, forbidden to him by his dentist; the detergent he used to have to carry back to his mother; the thick, embarrassing sanitary pads his sister once flashed him with from under her high-waisted underwear; the indispensable batteries that made the barking radios of war multiply and jingle, carrying breaking news while the city ground to a halt, that loquacious pause— and here he was in the dark, the only source of light a candle beneath a statue of the Virgin Mary with warm toes, feeding a child under her long blue robe, probably from a bottle of lukewarm water mixed with dried milk, and helping herself to the stack of diapers on the shelf above her, calmly rocking her angelic baby to the motion of the flickering flame. Pavlov's mother had often complained about the quality of the grocer's vegetables, and Pavlov himself had never approved of buying onions or garlic, or even the deep-red beets, because to his mind these were roots, and anything that had been buried underground should never be eaten.

He helped himself to two packs of his favourite cigarettes and a lighter, and when at last the grocer lifted the metal door, he faced the men on the sidewalk cracking jokes. One of them asked, Was it dark enough for you in there? How does it feel to be buried?

Pavlov calmly opened the pack of cigarettes, pulled out a smoke and lit it. He stood there eyeing the men, who were still laughing at him. Then he flicked the cigarette to the side of the road and grabbed one of the men by the collar. He lifted this man above his own head and suspended him in the air. The man began to scream, and his laughter and everyone else's ceased.

The grocer rushed towards Pavlov and begged him not to hurt the man. Pavlov lifted the man higher. Early on, he had learned from his father how to lift a corpse from the ground and deposit it in the back of the hearse. Now, he was perfectly composed as he lifted this living man. The other men stood unmoving, taken aback. Then, one after the other, they mumbled polite apologies and asked him to remain calm. Pavlov deposited the man on the roof of a nearby car, turned to face them and lit another cigarette.

There was silence as the man slowly clambered down from the car's roof. And in that moment of silence Pavlov decided that humans deserved their burials, their darkness and their extinction.

Over the next few weeks, the funeral processions under Pavlov's window alternated between those arranged for fighters who had been killed and those for civilians whose mourners hurried along the burial road in fear of falling bombs.

The remaining priest walked the road multiple times each day, repeating the same prayers, swinging his incense, which evaporated to make superfluous clouds shaped like pharaonic dogs and chariots carrying dead warriors. His companion, the dead priest, had been decimated by the bomb; his remains had been gathered in plastic bags and given to Pavlov's brute uncles to preserve until the clergyman's head could be located. But no one had been able to find that head yet.

On the day of the bomb, Pavlov had gone back to his balcony to retrieve the shoe, the toes and the ankle, with its heel, that had landed there. All these had belonged to the priest. He had lifted the ankle by the heel—Achilles' heel, he had thought. And then he'd repeated his joke out loud. A piece of broken tibia was sticking out, and a blood clot had already thickened and dotted the skin like measles. Pavlov noticed that the priest had tied the laces of his shoe in an X pattern, not the more sophisticated horizontal lines. Neglect, he murmured to himself. And an orphan, he deduced. The priest must have been a poor child who had learnt that life could go sideways all on his own. The diagonal X had survived the blow, though the front of the shoe was wide open and resembled a gaping fish that had lost its ocean, a pleading, quacking duck in the grip of a butcher, a panting dog, a feeding whale. This openness caused Pavlov to reflect, and more images came to his mind: open fields, open seas, open caskets, open thighs . . . He examined the shoelaces once more, firmly pulled and firmly tied. This headless priest had never learned how to properly lace a shoe, Pavlov concluded. And he must have been cautious, ever fearful that he would step on a loose lace and trip and fall into the burial pit. Pavlov sighed and shook his head. Knots were to be taken seriously, and those who knew how to use knots in battles and at sea had a better chance to conquer, advance and glide into the sunset, or the fortune of dragging their enemies' corpses behind their chariots.

All these years, Pavlov had never talked to the dismembered priest. It had been the still-living priest who came often to his father's business to collect the rent on the burial land, and to discuss ceremonies and other special arrangements for maintenance, digging and burial space. The now-headless priest, on the other hand, had not been mercenary. He had been more of an introvert, and consequently said little. People preferred him because he was laconic, which gave him an aura of contemplation and piety. The headless priest had also had the better singing voice, and he was handsome with his green eyes, his fair skin and his straight hair. Women loved him and sought his counsel. As a result, the line for confession had often been uneven between the two priests. The women confessed everything and anything to the headless priest except their love for him.

Once, in an Easter church procession, Pavlov had followed along behind the pagan re-enactment of the Virgin Mary weeping over the crucified Jew. Pierre, his cousin, had played a Roman soldier, holding a whip and lashing it at Jesus, who was dragging a wooden cross. Salwa the hyena, dressed in white, had followed her brother, her laughs muffled by the loud singing of the congregation. Suddenly, in a fit of madness, she had rushed at the green-eyed priest and thrown herself at his feet, grabbing his thighs, feeling his legs, screaming and wailing. She was hauled away by her father, Mounir, who dragged her behind the church wall. There he gave her a beating, until a few women rushed over to stop him, begging him to be calm and to forgive. They threw their bodies at him and held his hands away from his daughter. Then a few men ran over and pulled Mounir away.

Now, as the search for the priest's green-eyed head continued, the Christians in the city were petitioning to canonize him and honour his miraculous disappearance as well as his earlier acts of forgiveness and altruism. But the head of the priest was a prerequisite for the canonization request. A wandering soulless head was in conflict with the Church's teachings; to leave a body and a heart wandering without a mind was to court lust, debauchery and uncontrolled emotions. A heart without a head could easily fall into a life (or afterlife) of romantic pursuits and self-destructive behaviour.

And what if the devil had got hold of the priest's head, as Pavlov fancied? He might well be performing sacrilegious acts, such as kidnapping Europa while she was bathing, seducing Helen of Troy on a trip to Paris, converting Hellenic Zeus to fascism or monotheism.

The problem of the missing head presented a theological dilemma for the locals, and thus a contingent with good hearts were dispatched to search every corner of every street. They even went up to Pavlov's roof with keys he had provided. He listened to their aimless steps above him. His father had once kept pigeons on the roof, but recently Pavlov had cut the throats of three of them, plucked them, cooked them, eaten them and shared the leftovers with Rex the dog. The rest he had liberated and watched as they slowly migrated towards the trees of the cemetery before disappearing for a few days— although some of them, regardless of the killing, had returned.

Naturally, rumours spread that it was Pavlov who had hidden the head. If he could keep the left foot of the priest in his possession before handing it to the mournful congregation, why not the head? The head of a potential saint is a valuable thing to keep! Just imagine the conversations one might have with a bodiless priest. Imagine the theological arguments one could engage in, or the confessions, the wealth of confessions to disclose, a whole lexicon of debauchery and deceit, fear and regrets, petty stories of guilt and repentance.

Pavlov smiled at this. He imagined that such a head could, like Medusa's, turn a man into stone.

In any case, the priest's head was never found, and by July he was buried without it.

NADJA AGAIN

One night when the bombs were falling again, Pavlov took the stairs down to the street. He thought he might visit Nadja.

As he descended, a flickering light filled the stairwell of his house and the smell of incense floated up to him, reminding Pavlov of those small chapels he had been obliged to attend during his school days. When he reached the bottom step, he saw the Lady of the Stairs. Burning candles were everywhere—on the ground at the edge of the stair rail, on wooden boxes, and a trail of candles led all the way to the door. Pavlov paused for a moment. He asked the lady if she had gone out and bought these candles, but the lady just curled up where she sat, and hummed, and didn't look at him. He looked around for matches but could not see any of the telltale little sticks. He gently reached for the lady's hand, opened her fingers and smelled her palm—but there was no trace of fire or wood. He looked around again, this time for a lighter, but found nothing. At last, he left the lady and her candles, and started towards Nadja's place.

Pavlov walked all night. He went down the hill of Achrafieh, took the French stairs, passed the neighbourhood of Mar Mikhael and went straight towards the bridge, then crossed into the periphery of Bourj Hammoud. There, he traced his steps from the falafel place and found his way to the murder scene of the hooker and her pimp. He knocked, and Nadja opened the door. She recognized him and smiled.

He sat in her kitchen, and she offered him food. For a while, as he ate, they sat in silence.

Then Nadja spoke. Sometimes, people have no need to explain, talk or justify, she said. I like your silence. She touched his face. Do you want to stay?

Yes, he said.

Did you shower?

He shook his head, walked to her room and lay on her bed.

She laughed, and followed him.

That night, in Nadja's arms, he felt sad. He thought of the Lady of the Stairs and her candles, and of the mystery of the many fires in his home. At last, he fell asleep.

The next morning, he woke early, carefully liberated himself from Nadja's embrace, got dressed and went looking for the bathroom. The apartment was chopped up into small rooms and access to the bathroom was at the end of a tunnel-like corridor. The closed doors stood firm, guarding memories of lubricant, semen and single soft tissues drawn from a box by the bed.

The bathroom had a standing shower made of turquoise tiles separated by Cartesian lines that must have once glowed in their whiteness. All the towels looked wet and heavy, so Pavlov contented himself with whipping water from his palm against his face and then against his thighs. On the way back down the corridor he passed one of the ladies, who was groaning to herself over a cup of tea.

He remembered leaving his watch at the side of the bed, so re-entered Nadja's room on tiptoe, thinking to leave her some change—but Nadja was awake and watching him. In her morning voice, her eyes squinting, she told him not to bother. He had turned to go when he heard her speak again, with her French accent, asking why he hadn't wanted her to take off her clothes, why he didn't touch her.

Pavlov paused and looked back at Nadja, but didn't answer. He left without a word.

He walked back across the bridge and up the hill to the cemetery road. When he arrived at his house, the candles at the entrance had burned down. The wax had dripped and splattered and stretched with exhaustion, melting and surrounding the Lady of the Stairs, who was sound asleep.

REX

One early August morning as birds flew over the cemetery, leaving droppings on the crosses and stones, gliding past what was left of the early morning moon and chirping warnings to extraterrestrials who had dodged behind the lunar dune when the Americans had landed there, Pavlov made his way across the road to feed Rex, the dead warrior's dog. As he did so, he heard what sounded like an animal's cry coming from inside the cemetery. He jumped the fence and walked towards the noise, which alternated between small yelps and loud moaning. Slowly, he approached a large rock that stood at the far edge of the cemetery. His cousin Salwa was on her knees, her open palms flat on the ground, her knees mud-stained, the tips of her shoes slightly curved inwards and digging at the earth, her skirt raised, her blouse half-open, rocking back and forth in time to the young militiaman who had once aimed his rifle and shot at Pavlov's window.

Upon seeing Pavlov, the young man stopped his thrusting, but his cousin turned and looked up at him, slapping the boy's thigh repeatedly in the manner of a jockey on a racing horse, and Son of Mechanic proceeded with his fucking, oblivious once more to Pavlov's gaze. Salwa looked Pavlov straight in the eye and shrieked her loud laugh.

Pavlov turned and walked back towards the fence, climbed it and jumped down. His flight was not as graceful as that of Tariq the young fighter who had flown down to his death from the hotel, and the dog, who was waiting outside the fence, whimpered.

Pavlov recalled the day the bomb decimated the funeral procession, and how his cousin's laugh had caused him to walk over and slap her hard. She must already have had the son of the mechanic at her disposal. He was probably willing to do everything she asked—perhaps even kill a spectator watching from a window. What a man won't do from lust, thought Pavlov. Romantic love! Pavlov laughed at the thought, and Rex howled. Even Zeus, the son of Cronos, the God of Thunder, had been driven by Hera to take the Achaean side. And why not help the hyena take revenge? he asked the dog. I was the one who tried to stop her from laughing, that day of the bomb. But I was wrong. In fact, why not laugh? Laughter should be permissible under all circumstances, he now solemnly declared, and Rex nodded.

And why not laugh? the dog repeated. I blame those Semitic gods and their austere, sombre, humourless ways, Rex said. We canines, in ancient Egypt, were once revered as caretakers to the Gods. We were the custodians of the dead. And Rex laughed a human laugh.

Pavlov was reminded of his father's laughter, his sense of humour in the company of the dead. When Pavlov was a child, his father would take him to the morgue and show him the etiquette of knotting ties and the art of tying shoelaces. A tie, his father had preached one such day, should be tightened firmly around the neck, but a shoe knot can be left loose. The fellow is not going anywhere.

At this, his father had giggled; he enjoyed dressing up the dead. He brushed their hair, raised their torsos and lifted their necks to wrap them in white collars and formal ties. Powder and blush were puffed upon cadaverous cheeks to encourage the illusion of potential resurrection. His father had hummed while he worked, urging his bodies to relax and bear everything with patience. He would lift his head and smile at Pavlov, and once in a while ask him to shake the stiff's hand.

Look, son, see how perfect he is. All the fellow needs to do now is speak. Watch and learn, his father had told Pavlov. And then he had added: And those who don't have the chance to dress up and be buried—they will be taken by the winds and the burning sun.

GAS BONBONS

Pavlov hopped into his father's hearse, turned left and exited the cemetery road. He suddenly realized that he hadn't left the street for days. Yet he was satisfied with his routine, his immobility, his view of the passage of seasons over the headstones, his chain-smoking, and his conversations with Rex—all of which made him strangely content.

On his way out that morning, he had remembered to bring breakfast to the Lady of the Stairs. She still hadn't uttered a word since the day of the massacre, but now when he sat next to her, she touched his face, combed his hair with her fingers and smiled at him. With time comes progress, he declared to her. Then he'd walked out of the house, fed the dog and steered the hearse towards the highway. The city roads were almost empty under the falling bombs, which he ignored. Only an occasional fast car would pass by him in a flash. On the highway, he found himself behind a pickup filled with militiamen, their rifles pointing towards the sky. Some were wearing jeans, some had helmets and military boots, and others wore American baseball caps and cheap shoes. They were sitting in the back of the truck, in two rows facing each other, bouncing up and down with their rifles. Upon seeing Pavlov's car, some of the men crossed themselves and began shouting to their driver. The driver looked in his rear-view mirror and accelerated to get away from the omen of death.

Fearful that one of the soldiers would shoot at him, Pavlov accelerated too, and tried to pass the militia truck, but the driver blocked his way and the men in the back jeered at him, raising their fists and aiming their guns at his windshield. To escape their wrath and superstition, Pavlov took the next exit, which veered towards the neighbourhood of Dawra. He passed a bus terminal, the drivers in sandals busy fanning flies and luring passengers. Trucks in this area bore bold prophecies on stickers slapped on their doors and trunks: *This is what God bestowed on me and may the jealous guy get a stick in the eye.*

For a while, Pavlov followed a slow bus, reading the sign on its rear: *Do not speed, Father, for death is faster.* He repeated this a few times, laughing, singing the phrase in an incantation: *Do not speed, Father, for death is faster.*

Pavlov was used to the reaction towards his deathmobile. When, in his childhood, his father had driven the family out of the city towards the mountains or along the seashore with its wavy beaches—past salty restaurants with hay roofs shading straw chairs that had been woven by blind pupils in orphanages and charity homes—an uneasiness would settle on the road as they passed. Other cars would distance themselves from the family's long black vehicle; some even stopped and changed direction. The deathmobile was the family car, and alternated between carrying the dead and carrying the family to the rare social events to which an undertaker was invited. Once, when they arrived at a cousin's wedding, the groom became furious. As Pavlov's family stepped out of the hearse in their Sunday clothes, the father of the bride crossed himself and a relative of the groom hurried over with incense in her hands, circling the car and mumbling prayers. The bride remained hidden in the kitchen with the windows shuttered, and then two cousins of the groom came out of the house, threatened Pavlov's father with violence and asked him to leave.

Pavlov's sister had turned red from embarrassment. She shed tears, and the makeup on her face melted and rushed down her cheeks and dripped off her chin, staining her dress. Pavlov had watched silently as his sister's fingers clutched her fake-leather handbag while his mother started to ululate, wishing the bride happiness, until his father put a hand over his mother's mouth and pushed her back inside the car. They turned around and drove back towards the cemetery road.

Today, as Pavlov drove, he passed people on the streets hurrying among the few stores where owners were still selling merchandise through small gaps under their metal doors before the bombing resumed. By now, he thought, the people of Lebanon should be used to the sight of his long black vehicle of death with its high, grey-roofed top and tinted windows. At the very least, they should have accepted its necessity alongside all the killing and death. But our utilitarian species,

Pavlov thought, only tolerates my kind when faced with their own bereavement. He drove farther, taking narrow streets until he reached the highway again. Then he continued along the coastline ravaged by warlords, who had confiscated the sand and the waterfront for their corrupt building projects. On his trips with his father to the cremation house, his father would rant as they drove along the coast: Ugly hotels, he might say, depriving access to swimmers and bathers and the original inhabitants of the land. Those greedy contractors and their lovers, those beneficiaries of shady deals, have ruined the beaches . . .

Pavlov pulled over outside a factory on the shoreline. There, he bought two industrial-size propane tanks and ten metres of pipe and some bolts. A little farther along, he also stopped at a grocery and bought food—some loaves, tea, sugar, a bottle of whisky, fruit, and bones for the dog. And before getting into his car again, he went back inside to buy some chocolates for the Lady of the Stairs.

He drove up into the mountains, instinctively finding his way to the cremation house. When he arrived, he lifted the vase under which the key rested, alongside the vermin who had made the bottom of the dead plant their home. He unlocked the door and stepped inside.

Inside, the rooms were damp and cold, and the walls were deteriorating. But blocks of wood waited by the stove, and on the bed was a book. Sometimes, while a body was burning in the furnace, his father would read. And sometimes he would recite, under his breath, passages by heart. Pavlov picked up the book, but he didn't recognize the language in which it was written. His father had made notes in the margin, and drawings that looked like circles and divisions. Pavlov peered more closely: they were drawings of serpents and stars.

He walked around the house, looking for clues. He opened the cupboards and drawers, and checked under the sink. Finally he lifted the mattress on the bed and found books underneath. He flipped through them; they all seemed to be in different languages. Some had beautiful illustrations— drawings of lions, a child, a woman—and from what Pavlov could make out, Latin and Syriac text. His father had scribbled in Arabic in the margins, *Sophia*.

Pavlov lit the wood in the stove, heated some food and ate. He lay on his father's bed and drank from a bottle of whisky. The books were a mystery. They were old and strange. They had been read repeatedly, judging by the stains on the pages and the cracks in their spines.

Father, he said. Father, what are you?

He slept deeply. The next morning, waking early, he started work on the crematorium. He locked the gas faucet, removed the old propane tanks and examined the pipes, which were starting to show signs of fissures and cracks. He followed their trajectories through the opening of a small metal door and beneath the furnace. He cut them and pulled them out. By noon, he had attached the canisters, which his father had always called bonbons, to the new bolts on the ends of the pipes, securing a stream of gas to the furnace.

Fearing a leak, he opened the windows. Then he lit the furnace and a burst of flames flared immediately. He could regulate the flow of gas by twisting the bonbons' opening and using the faucet in the wall, and now he watched the heat transform from red to purple to a dark blue.

He let the furnace run, and went outside to smoke and gaze at the steep hills. As he stood there, he noticed the outline of a narrow road. He stubbed out his cigarette and walked along the winding path, registering the passage of time by the growth of trees in front of steep rocks.

Upon reaching the end of the road at the edge of a cliff, he took a handful of dust and let it drop. The dust flew back in his face and he swallowed it. As he coughed and spat, he recalled his father's knowledge of the wind and its directions. His father would stand at the edge of the cliff and sniff the air before pouring the deceased into the valley.

The sun was now above the mountains and the valley was covered in a haze of heat. By the time Pavlov had returned to the house, he was covered in sweat. A sense of melancholy settled over him, and he wiped his brow with the back of his arm.

The house's interior was boiling. Every object bore the heat of the furnace. The books that he gathered to put back under the bed seemed crisper, and some of the pages had curled, making letters rise and fall in their landscape of mysterious words. He shut off the bonbons and the faucet, and opened the oven's door. A blaze of heat hit him in the face. Sweat rolled down his forehead, ran over his eyes and settled above his lips. The heat was comforting, and soon he couldn't tell if it was sweat that poured from his eyes or tears.

He gathered what was left of his food but left the bottle of whisky. Then he locked the door and replaced the key under the vase.

TOWARDS THE BOMBED CITY

Pavlov drove back towards the war. He passed through villages and small towns, his long hearse coursing down the curving roads of steep valleys. Death, he reminded himself, also existed at this altitude. Sometimes there were flights off the cliffs by drivers who lost control—drunk urbanites in search of small restaurants with authentic cuisine who filled their bellies and drove, intoxicated by the alcohol and the fresh air, experiencing a last ride in their shiny machine before plummeting into the valleys.

Pavlov passed little shrines housing bearded saints, statues planted like flowers where sleepy drivers had experienced the last surges of their existence, crosses marking the final curves for those who couldn't hang on to the road as their headlights beamed into the quiet drop below. Pavlov drove his deathmobile through this orbit of accidents. Locals don't fly off the roads, he mused. They are born to this terrain, to the sloping sky and steep valleys. They are born with goats' feet, like mischievous Pan, their hooves conveniently curved, their eyes shining at night under the brilliance of the howling moon, their thick fingers matching the knotted tree roots and rocks. When they climb, they hunch their backs; when they descend, they lean forwards and dangle their heads into the abyss. But reckless city dwellers, living like rodents in Beirut—they are forever distracted by their mirrors, by perfume in the glove compartment, by the luscious thighs of their passengers, as they roll down the speedy hills. And when they spin off the road, they hover briefly in their best casual attire, their ties suspended parallel to their tongues, and their scent leaves a trail of sweetness and a whiff of the coming fall. And as the car plunges, its tail lights paint a red line above the darkened valley, and afterwards, loud music bangs on through the early morning like the underwater sound of aquatic mammals. When the early risers in the village spot the smoke and smell the gasoline, they follow the music that echoes through the valley. They rush to the cliffs early on Sundays before the tolling of bells and the resurrection of smoke. There they gather and cross themselves, shaking their heads and murmuring to each other: *city folk, city folk.*

Pavlov amused himself with these thoughts as he drove towards the bombed city. Cars rushed past in the other direction, seeking to avoid the bombs—but Pavlov knew that these drivers increased their chance of death when they accelerated in fear. One should be as cool as ice, he reflected as the bombs fell ahead and behind, and he saw uprisings of grey smoke from mortars landing on the roofs of nearby houses and shops. He concentrated on the road ahead, briefly noting a long cement wall covered in war slogans—*The Bats passed by here*; *Christians Forever*—and cedar-shaped triangles, badly painted, punctuating these slogans at intervals. He read all this quickly as he drove by, leaving the signs and words of this world behind, remaining composed while the bombs fell around him.

As he crossed the Nahr bridge, he was as patient as a war refugee occupying the slums of the earth in a house made of cardboard; and he was patient as he watched animal-shaped clouds resting outside his windshield. He drove slow and calm, eyeing the clouds as they drifted and changed into monsters and other fleeting creatures.

NADJA ONCE MORE

B y mid-August, a ceasefire was declared, and the passage of the dead along the cemetery road slowed. Pavlov lingered at home, reading the Greeks and smoking. He fed Rex and, from above, watched the dog welcoming the rare funeral procession. The dead who passed below his window these days were mostly older people, and their funerals tended to be less noisy, more expected. If tearful outbursts arose, they elicited condemnation from bystanders, as if excessive sadness for the passing of the elderly was an indulgence. The young have died by the dozen, some of the bystanders said. These deceased had full lives and we should be grateful they have lived so long.

During this time, Pavlov's brute uncles came to inquire again about the deathmobile. The elder, Maurice, said that he had heard from high-ranking sources in the militia that the ceasefire would not last long, and another fierce battle was imminent. They would need the hearse for their business.

The younger, Mounir, reminded Pavlov of their contract, and tried to shame him by invoking the name of his father. My brother would have disapproved, Mounir said, repeating the word *brother* multiple times. My brother, may he rest in peace!

The car is off limits, Pavlov replied simply. And you still owe me and my sister money from the sale of our share of the business.

What about that woman living at the bottom of your stairs? his uncles asked angrily. Is she your whore?

Pavlov violently pushed his uncles out of the house.

The next morning, Pavlov was standing on his balcony. Son of Mechanic approached and stood looking up at him, his gun visible at his waist, his shoulders pumped from his military training. He pointed at Pavlov with his index finger and clicked an imaginary gun with his thumb, then touched and thrust his groin in a vulgar manner.

Pavlov fixed his eyes on him, moving his gaze only to light a cigarette.

Finally, Son of Mechanic walked away, shaking his head menacingly.

That afternoon, Pavlov got into his car and drove east towards the neighbourhood of Naba'a. He turned into a small street, parked, and went up to a yellow building with green French shutters. He entered and climbed the stairs to the top floor. One of the hookers—he couldn't remember her name—answered his knock. She was blonde and had blue eyes and spoke in broken Arabic.

Is Nadja here? he asked.

It's not a good time now. Come tomorrow.

Tell her it's Pavlov.

Wait.

After a moment Nadja appeared. It's good to see you, she said.

Pavlov nodded.

Well, come in. The girls are making dinner.

The smell of food filled the apartment. In the kitchen, three women ignored him and kept cooking. The music was loud and they sang along to it.

I was about to take a shower, Nadja said. You can go to my room. I'll be there soon.

He walked along the corridor to Nadja's room. He sat in the chair in the corner and stared at the bed, feeling miserable. He could justify neither staying nor going. He looked at his shoes and contemplated taking them off.

Nadja entered. She wore no makeup and her feet were bare, and she looked small and pale, wrapped in a towel.

She lay on the bed and asked him to join her.

He took off his shoes and lay down beside her. She smelled of shampoo and her wet hair turned everything she touched moist.

Where have you been? she asked. And how is the burial business?

Everyone wants a fanfare, Pavlov said quietly.

Nadja replied, They want to bid farewell with dignity.

There is no dignity for the dead. There are only ceremonies for the living.

Comforting the living at the hour of departure is an act of love, Nadja said.

They kissed, and then Nadja removed her towel. She untied his belt and pants and moved her mouth towards his groin. She brushed her lips above his pubic hair, breathing on it, and drew semicircles in brief kisses on his inner thighs, one of her hands pushed against his stomach, almost piercing the skin with her red nails. Her other hand circled his erection, bending him to the side. She teased him for a while, glancing from below at his face and, as their eyes met, closing her eyelids quickly with a playful bashfulness. Then her lips opened again, and she pushed down the skin of his uncircumcised penis, exposing the mushroom top. She took it in her mouth and sucked it fast, then slowed, looking at his face, her strokes alternating speed and power. With her free hand she pushed the veil of hair from her face back over her shoulders, and looked up into his eyes.

Her gaze was fearless now, bolder the more she sucked him—assertive, even confrontational. She took charge, dominating him, pressing her lips hard against his, and pushed him back on the bed, locking his wrists together over the pillow.

Repeat after me: I am going to surrender, and let go. Just say that, she told him. When he stayed silent, she said, Fine.

She went to the window and removed the red ribbon

tie-backs from the curtains. These she used to fasten his hands together tightly above the white sheets. Then she caressed him and kissed his chest, neck and lips. She went down on him, then looked up again. She stopped, seemingly hesitant at all the choices open to her. At last, she took his penis and guided it inside her. She moved back and forth, slowly at first, then steadily increasing the tempo into violent fucking. The metal bed squeaked loudly. She slowed, looked him in the eye and smiled an affectionate smile. She kissed his mouth.

Pavlov, she said. What a fitting name for a man who likes to observe the repetitive gestures of others. She whispered this, and her voice recalled the conversations of sad creatures conspiring in hushed tones, in good faith, across bloodstained tables or dangerous rooms, across dirty sheets.

Now she walked her knees over his stomach, his chest, and positioned the lips of her vagina on his face and nostrils.

Pavlov stretched his tongue clumsily, without aim, seemingly missing everything. She adjusted herself and pressed downwards, then rocked forwards and back, making his lips open wide as he gasped for breath.

Breathe, she instructed him. Breathe and I will untie you.

When she did finally untie him, he stood up, a little bashful, contemplating violence towards her. He hesitated, his palm open, and looked at his ring; it was the only one he had kept from his father's collections of jewellery from the dead. He twisted it.

But Nadja sensed his intention and said, It was just a game. You take captivity too seriously. If anything, surrender will liberate you from the burden of yourself.

He wanted to leave, but she held his hand and said, You should have come more often. I like your sad self. I always want something different with you . . . And now I have to think about leaving the country. I think I am done here. The war is too dangerous for a foreigner like me. This place is lawless, and the men take off their belts and lay their guns on the table, even before taking off their shoes. If I leave, and if you ever decide to move from this place, please find me.

Pavlov was unsure how to respond. He placed all the money in his pocket on the table, and left.

MOTHER, GRANDMOTHER

In the morning, Pavlov went across the road as usual to buy cigarettes. Two bearded militiamen were standing in the grocer's doorway, eating sandwiches and drinking Pepsi. Their breath reeked of killing. They submerged themselves in their food, parting the bread with big bites, leaning their heads sideways to watch everything. They kept an eye on their jeeps, the guns at their waists and the women who passed by.

They want to be seen, Pavlov observed. They want to be feared and revered, and they will offer their bodies, their blood, to the earth and its diggers, in return for a heroic tale. Real killers should be willing to be killed. That's the deal, Pavlov thought. That's the pact they make with life. And a fair game that is.

Pavlov wondered whether he would eventually turn into a killer himself. Would he one day take his father's gun and point it at Son of Mechanic and pull the trigger?

He caught himself staring at the weapon of one of the fighters. The fighter glanced back. Do you like this? he asked, pointing at the handgun at his waist.

My father had one just like it, Pavlov replied.

Is it for sale? asked the fighter.

It's already sold, Pavlov said.

The fighter nodded and chewed and watched Pavlov, and knew he was lying. But he was also flattered. He enjoyed having his gun noticed.

The fighters hardly used their guns in battle. They were for show and status, and were mostly brought out in close combat. Handguns were meant to be waved at comrades, and at allies when they ceased to be allies, not used on enemies who remained far away and out of the pistol's reach.

Pavlov had handled a handgun before. His brute uncle Maurice had showed him how to use one. This was when Pavlov's father was still alive and everyone in the family was pretending to fall into line and love each other. Once in a while during those times, the family would drive a convoy of deathmobiles up to the mountains for a picnic. They would start a fire and bring out the meat and meze. That was when Uncle Maurice had taught Pavlov how to fill a handgun's chamber with bullets, then crank it and aim it at cans and empty bottles.

Pavlov walked away before the fighter had finished eating. He wondered what killers do after they are done killing, and why no one from the militia had approached him to join up. All the young men around him had been slowly lured and recruited into the militia. But no one had approached the undertaker's son. A legion of cadavers protected him, and his father's thick eyebrows, thick hands, quiet manner and laconic nature had made people uneasy around the family. And then there was his mother, Josephine—the wild woman, as everyone had called her. She had been shunned by the world, always wearing a black dress, always loud and vulgar in her manners and in her madness—her mental illness and her fits and her delusional episodes. Her madness had begun on a deceptively calm morning. She had awakened the neighbourhood with her loud screams as she pointed at the cadavers. *The voices of the dead!* she had screamed. And from then on she had complained of their scent on her husband's clothing, on his breath and his hands that touched the dead and fumbled across her body.

The dead are everywhere, they are walking in the cemetery, they are coming to snatch our children, she would scream, and she would tear off her clothes and run to hide in the bathroom. She suffered a breakdown, and ended up in the psychiatric hospital. A classic case of depressive disorder, the doctor said. Pavlov's father would often repeat this as he wandered around the house, muttering, Your mother has a bad case of mental disorder.

Who in their right mind would live in the middle of a cemetery? the neighbours whispered, with their viper-like tongues.

When Pavlov's father had met her, Josephine was living with her mother in a small apartment under the stairs in a three-storey building. Josephine had a limp, and her feet curved inwards, and her smile revealed long black teeth. She and her mother shared one room with a tiny stove, and a tiny bathroom. The door of the apartment opened right onto the street. In the summer, Josephine and her mother would sit on low chairs between the parked cars that blocked the entrance to their home. Pavlov's grandmother sold cigarettes, tissues and chewing gum through the open window that gave onto the street. She wore an apron, whether she was cooking or not, and plastic slippers in all seasons, exposing the resilience of her toes, and she carried a lit cigarette that hardly left her lips. Smoke had shut one of her eyes like a buccaneer. She was loud, she cursed and spat on the ground like a pimp, and she fought with the owners of the cars that parked too close to her door, impeding her entrance or exit. The exhaust from these cars had stained the walls inside the house, as well as the hair and clothing of mother and daughter. She constantly fought with men and threatened them by waving her slippers in the air and calling upon the names of warrior saints to curse them.

Then one day Pavlov's grandmother fell from her chair and never woke up. She died in her apron, a cigarette still burning on her lips. It was Pavlov's father who noticed the daughter, and he fell in love with her. He took care of all the funeral arrangements for free, and he sent Josephine flowers. He bought her a new dress and shoes and invited her to his house. He courted her for forty days, and then they went straight to the priest and got married. Josephine refused to take off her black dress of mourning. Sabah, a church regular, stood as her witness, and Maurice, the elder of the brute brothers, stood as witness to Pavlov's father.

Pavlov's grandmother was buried across from the window of his home, under a pink granite headstone that Josephine could spot at a glance. Pavlov would often catch his mother talking to the pink stone and smoking, making an offering of cigarettes. Then one day her mumbling became prolonged, and the flaming cigarettes turned into razors that Josephine used on her own arms. She would stab herself with glowing embers and run naked towards the pink stone, screaming *Audette, Audette*—her mother's name. The burns left round spots on her arms and legs, releasing a smell of seared flesh that Pavlov, as a child, had imagined to be an offering to the gods.

Look, the dead are coming back towards us, his mother would say, pointing at the cemetery. Look, she would say, they are laughing at my mother, they are stealing her cigarettes. The guy who never paid us and the big guy over there still come to visit her at night. I used to see them moving under my mother's quilt, and moaning and rocking, and the few bills that guy used to leave under the dish rack he now lays on the edge of the stone. Look, he's helped himself to a pack again and he's smoking outside the gate and looking at us. He's eyeing your sister, dear Pavlov, hide her, hide . . .

One day, Josephine reached for a large kitchen knife and ran towards the cemetery gate. There she delivered a monologue to an invisible man in a tweed jacket who was holding a keychain and pointing to her mother's bed. Your daughter has grown, was his reply to Pavlov's mother. She has grown, Mashallah. At that, Josephine swung the knife in the direction of the sycamore tree, stabbing at the shadow it cast on the crosses.

It was only when Pavlov's mother turned her cigarette stabbing on her children that his father took her away and had her locked up. The nuns welcomed her in and kept her in a room in a monastery up in the mountains. Josephine disappeared for a few years, and then one day she showed up again, with prayer beads in hand, planting Virgin Marys and hanging crosses on every wall. She was in love with Mary now, and had forgiven the man who had slept in her mother's bed, and touched her—the fat man who, when she passed him on her way to the bathroom, would brush his organ against her, reciting under his filthy breath, Mashallah you have grown. For a time, Pavlov's household was in the service of the Virgin Mary—Mary blessed be her name this and Virgin Mary that—until slowly Mary's name was forgotten and all that was left were icons, relics of saints and crosses on the walls.

Over time, Josephine began to take care of the business side of the household. She turned away from the worship of a virgin goddess towards the worship of the mercantile Baal. Her offerings became price lists and an unparalleled variety of expensive coffins. She started to make flower arrangements for the dead. She mastered the choice of pillows, wood, funeral wreaths. She would note the name to appear on the wreath, and Nathalie would invent the most affectionate phrases to be written diagonally across the ribbons—an arrangement that made Pavlov think of the Greek letter pi.

This was the happiest time that Pavlov remembered from his youth—the time after his mother had accepted the dead and surrounded her family with decorative objects. At night over dinner, conversation about the choice of coffins brought intimacy to the table. On her deathbed, she asked Pavlov's father to bury her in the same spot as her mother, under the pink stone. She had picked her favourite coffin in cherrywood finish with delicate brass handles. And she asked him to bury her at night—so that no one would attend the funeral but the priest, their children and the Virgin Mary.

RESURRECTION

Pavlov was hungry, so he walked to Abou-Antoun's restaurant at the other end of the cemetery road. Abou-Antoun made arguably the best foul and hummus in the region. But the man was loquacious—he never shut the fuck up.

Pavlov sat and listened, just as all the men there sat and listened. Abou-Antoun was capable of cooking and talking nonstop behind his counter from dawn until afternoon, when he packed up and left.

I learned to close early, Abou-Antoun said, because it's a killing field behind us. I heard that some evenings those militia boys bring people and shoot them right behind us in that field. Sometimes I see the burned cadavers, but the next day they disappear. I don't know who picks them up. Someone in the neighbourhood said he saw a man picking them up all by himself. This man said the collection of the bodies was done by some kind of organization that will bury anyone, regardless of their religion or their past.

Pavlov stood up, paid the man and left. He arrived home to find that his front door was broken, and to his horror the Lady of the Stairs had been beaten. She had a black eye and cowered in the stairwell, small and quiet. When she saw Pavlov, she cried and released little muffled screams. Pavlov tried to talk to her, but it was hopeless. He rushed upstairs. His house was in disarray, and the little furniture he owned had been turned upside down. His books were thrown on the floor, and even the kitchen drawers had been removed and his utensils scattered on the ground.

He rushed downstairs with ice and bandages, held the Lady of the Stairs in his arms, and applied ice to her face. Then he carried her upstairs and laid her in his bed, where she stretched herself out under the covers and slept. Pavlov went back outside to his brute uncles' house, and stood outside the door. He began to pace back and forth, waiting for his family to see him and witness his rage. He was drooling with anger. At last he banged on the door, but no one answered. He picked up a rock and threw it at the door, then picked up another and threw it at a window and broke it. Still no one came out.

He walked towards the cemetery gates, found Rex the dog and paced around—and Rex talked to Pavlov. First, Rex tried to calm him down. Then he told Pavlov that humans were beyond help. He recalled theriomorphism, theriophily and Diogenes, who slept in a bathtub, barked at people and tried to imitate the manner of dogs. But you, Pavlov, Rex said, courted me out of admiration for my warrior master, who leapt to his death from a grand height. What a Spartan, a flying Spartan! Rex said. He wondered if his past master had experienced regret or sorrow during his fatal descent. The wind must have been overwhelmed by the weight of such a presence, the wind must have parted and retreated. Suicide, the dog continued, is the most heroic act, which no animal save for man dares to commit or could ever contemplate.

When the dog had finished lamenting, Pavlov left him at the gate of the cemetery and returned home.

That night, he tried sleeping in his bathtub, periodically climbing out to check on the woman in his bed. The next morning, he brought her food. She ate, and for the next two days slept in his bed and kept him company. As Pavlov fell asleep next to the Lady of the Stairs, she would look at him and burst out laughing. On the third night, they were woken by bombs falling close by. The Lady of the Stairs stood up, took off her clothes and walked out into the living room, so Pavlov took off his pyjamas and followed her. They both laughed at the musicality of the explosions, the faint smell of rain, the moonlight that passed through the window and fell upon their nakedness. The shower of bombs made them hysterical, and they started to dance and then to re-enact scenes of killing, mocking death, burial and resurrection. And then Pavlov pretended to be a flying horse, and the Lady of the Stairs, in the manner of heroes and prophets, sat on his back and flew to heaven. They slow-danced, brushing their genitals against one another, clumsily stepping on each other's toes, lightly touching each other's thighs and buttocks. They walked around the room on hands and feet, sniffing each other's behinds and howling.

Silly humans, Pavlov whispered, the things they believe.

The things they believe, the lady repeated.

You talk! Pavlov said, overjoyed. Talk some more.

But she pushed him away, giggling, and started to dance alone. Her breasts were small and her nipples rosy, her toes round and light on the ground, with a gradual reduction in size from big toe to the smallest, slicing the marble floor at a side angle. Her shoulders were two small, pointy bones that stood out beneath her skin. Her round hips and luscious thighs made Pavlov pursue her in the manner of an unabashed canine.

In bed, she laughed at him and said, Resurrection. She laughed again and turned away, wrapping herself in the heavy quilt, and went back to sleep.

Resurrection, Pavlov repeated, as he lay on his back panting, smiling with another erection under the weight of the cover. He recalled a burial he had witnessed when he was little. He had been standing between the priest and his father. Everyone had been looking down at the grave while the priest swung the incense burner and promised resurrection. Pavlov had asked the priest if the dead would be resurrected naked or wearing clothes. The priest gave him a severe look, but his father had beamed a triumphant smile, proud of his son.

In his youth, Pavlov had thought often of Resurrection. It had consumed him—the idea of the flight upwards. At the sound of the largest bell in the universe, the bell of the Second Coming, Pavlov had imagined he would surely be standing at the window, facing the cemetery, as the earth started to crack open. He would intone, Dust and sand shall mushroom upwards! The stones and crosses of the earth would topple, and millions of cadavers, all naked, would dust themselves off with their bony hands, brushing their skulls with the tips of their fingers. They would form two separate lines—the good and the sinful—and begin an ascent towards the open sky, or a descent into hell. A small flood would be sent by the jealous Yahweh, Pavlov had assumed, to cleanse the muddy bodies. The good would then scrub themselves before their celestial departure, and naked women with clean, tender skin would form a migration of flying beauties, restored to their youth. All wounds, headaches, menstrual cramps, bad hairdos, chagrin, money troubles and petty inconveniences would be erased, and the resurrected would take flight towards Jesus, guided by Buraq, the flying horse, to lands of milk and honey, and new beginnings . . .

Ha-ha, Pavlov laughed, and fell into a coma-like slumber.

───

The next morning, Pavlov heard the first tuning note of the brass band. He climbed out of bed. Another shortened life, he thought. Too soon, too fast, had death come to it. He hummed the rest of the brass band's tune.

He washed his face, fluffed his curly hair, grabbed his round glasses, changed his clothes, faced the window and waited for the procession to appear. All the stories of the dead now seemed ordinary to him. The trope of war had been played and replayed since Homer—a play for the Gods to observe from on high. And if humans were not being manipulated by Olympian gods, they were manipulating each other for their own ends. What a naive species we are, Pavlov thought. The stories we die for.

As the wedding procession for the young dead began, he felt the Lady of the Stairs standing next to him. She, too, was looking down—at the women in black, who walked slowly along on the cemetery road.

In a low voice the Lady of the Stairs said, Now I remember everything. And I must leave.

Without a glance at him or a trace of sadness, she went to the bedroom, covered her body and feet in her black clothing, and walked out of Pavlov's house. Pavlov stood at the window and watched her walking against the flow of black, back to the end of the road's beginning. There she stopped once, turned back, threw Pavlov a look and a modest smile, and disappeared.

REX AGAIN

Pavlov slept well that night.

The woman is gone, he reflected, before falling asleep. It had taken the musicality of death for her to remember death. At this thought, he felt regret in his heart. The last few days, and her playfulness and laughter, had made him happy. The few encounters he'd had with women had always been fleeting. Courtship stressed him: the interruption of his private thoughts, the need to pay attention to others, the tragic, grotesque, serious business of love, the idea of possession as well as procreation—all these horrified him. Existence was his exile and nothingness was his home.

He reminded himself that a dog might grieve the loss of companions but did not care for the ceremonies of the living for the dead.

He was woken in the night by nearby gunshots. Alarmed, he looked for his slippers by the dim light of a candle. But by the time he had found them and made up his mind to open his balcony door, quiet had returned. All seemed calm except for the sound of faraway explosions.

In the morning, he urinated inside the yellow-stained ring of the toilet bowl. Saturn, Saturn, he sang, and then he laughed and praised the ringed planet as he brushed his teeth in a circular motion. He opened the curtains and the sun came in. He boiled coffee on his little gas stove, and went downstairs to feed the dog. He opened his door and there was Rex, shot, his body lying on the gravel road, decapitated.

He closed the door.

Then he ran upstairs, grabbed a garbage bag and returned to his front doorstep. He put the remains of the headless dog in the bag, carried it to his kitchen, emptied his fridge, put the dog in it and walked towards his uncles' house. He paced back and forth in front of the building. He approached the front door and knocked violently. Again no one answered. He threw stones at the entrance and waited, and finally made his way back home.

After a while, he walked to the grocer's to buy candles and ice. The grocer was out of candles. Your laughing cousin bought them all the other night, the man said.

Pavlov bought a six-pack of ice. He carried it home and emptied it over Rex's remains. Have you ever seen that hyena inside her house lighting candles? he asked the dog, but Rex could no longer shake his head.

That night, Pavlov sat on his balcony and waited. He watched and listened. He didn't eat. He drank water and smoked. Then he howled at the full moon. He howled for the longest time, calling to the head of his dog. He howled until his throat burned, wondering all the while when, exactly, his hyena cousin had managed to enter his house and light up his stairwell with her small candle flames.

He drank a glass of water to soothe his throat from all the howling.

Water, Pavlov thought, as he held the glass in his left hand. Death by water was intriguing—and the idea of sailing away from this inhospitable place consumed his thoughts. The sea could be a good burial site for the dead, he considered—but then he was troubled by thoughts of his mother, and all the fluids that must have escaped her body during his birth. He thought about that stage when a body turns to liquid inside a closed casket while the bones linger for a while longer, before, finally, there is liberation, and the evaporation of the dust. Then he remembered the Lady of the Stairs, her silent affection, her gestures, her madness and caresses that had made him feel whole, and Rex the dog's wagging tail each morning, and the routines that grounded him and made him briefly withdraw from his solitary existence to join the cycle of life—some cycle, any cycle.

And suddenly the night pulled in more darkness, and Pavlov prepared to howl once again.

FALL

SOCIETY BUSINESS

Early one September evening, two strangers dressed in leather jackets and pants, and high boots, showed up at Pavlov's door. They introduced themselves as Hanneh and Manneh, and said that El-Marquis had sent them to assist with Society matters.

May we come in? they asked.

Pavlov ushered them in, and they went straight upstairs.

Both men wore thick eyeliner and red lipstick. Their hair was long and, Pavlov noted, a bit greasy from their helmets—helmets that each now held against his ribs, on opposite sides, accentuating the symmetry of their appearance.

Manneh withdrew a stack of money and placed it on the table. Both men looked around the house, then peered out of the window and up at the sky. They stepped out onto the balcony and glanced at the cemetery.

Manneh went to the kitchen and came back with a bottle of water. He drank from it and handed it to Hanneh.

Let's go, Manneh said, addressing Pavlov.

Bring some identification, Hanneh said. The militia at the checkpoints don't like bikers or long hair.

They put on their helmets and went downstairs.

——

Pavlov rode behind Manneh as they drove down the hill and towards the seashore. Pavlov had no helmet, and his curly hair sucked up, trapped and filtered particles like the sponges that his father had used to scrub the unmoving faces of cadavers.

They drove past Achrafieh's maze of little shops and houses, and Pavlov was familiar with every curve and sidewalk on the narrow streets. Once the motorcycles reached the Nahr district, they made a left towards Quarantina and followed the highway towards the north. They left behind cars and trucks, raising dust as they moved. Pavlov had the taste of the city in his mouth. He looked over at a truck driver, and saw him singing—but the man's smile at Pavlov was cut short by the sudden acceleration of Manneh's motorcycle.

At length, they arrived at a restaurant on the beach. Manneh and Hanneh parked their vehicles and ushered Pavlov inside, where plastic chairs and tables with cheap nylon covers sat at the end of a cement pier, above the water. A woman in a yellow dress with a broad yellow hat on her head appeared like a crucifix against the blue backdrop of the ocean. Pavlov was reminded of the Swedish flag.

Pavlov, the woman said. She approached him with the slow gait of a tragic Nordic actress. Behind her, over the water, a plastic bag riding the many winds of the sea seemed indecisive about its final destination, full of air and sound, while a seagull on a mission from some god screamed profanity and insults at the world.

The woman reached for Pavlov's hand and escorted him to her kingdom above the water. She held his hand tightly, perhaps fearing that the wind might take him.

Pavlov, she said, repeating his name. She seemed to enjoy repeating it. Is that your militia name, your war name?

He shook his head.

I am asking only because many of the young fighters assume a borrowed name these days. I was told it has something to do with the communication devices they use. But maybe it is also because they are ashamed of who they are?

She led him to a plastic chair. He sat and leaned against the fragile table. The smell of the sea, the moving open ocean with its battered rocks and abundant algae, made him think of living things—things that arrive and then retreat. He heard the woman's voice again and was brought back to her kingdom above the sea.

In any case, it's an original name to have, Pavlov. I am so glad you came. My name is Souad by the way—not as original a name as yours—and I am a friend of El-Marquis. I understand he visited you at home. Actually, El-Marquis is my second cousin and we have known one another since birth. Well, I hope you don't mind, I already ordered us some food. The fish is coming. This place is a hidden gem—do not tell anyone about it, you know how people are. (She laughed.) The food is superb here. It is the grandmother who cooks . . . The daughter serves. It's a family business . . . The meal will come soon . . . I hope you like it . . . It is from fishermen down the coast . . . They pull the nets . . . *Jaroufee* they call it, you know.

Dear Pavlov, here's what I would like you to do. Money is not an issue. Like El-Marquis, I am dying. El-Marquis and I, strangely enough, we have the same disease at the same time— a family inheritance, and we are both dying. We sat together the other day and remembered our childhoods . . . Unlike El-Marquis, I grew up poor and I wanted to escape poverty at any price, so I married a rich old man. Money permitted my cousin to live a life of debauchery and transgression, but I decided to marry for money. Marrying a poor young man required, I thought then, much more effort and the risk of continuous poverty. But life taught me differently . . . Well, my dear Pavlov, this is my story and why I wanted to meet with you, you see.

Upon my death, my children will bury me with their father, an awful tyrant who abused me for my entire married life—and I am afraid he will continue to do so, from the grave, after my death. Yes, I agreed to marry him even though he was older than me by thirty years. You see, I was young and beautiful and thought I needed someone to take care of me. Back then, I had long, straight dark hair and big eyes.

After our marriage, after our first sexual encounter, I found my husband repulsive . . . and with time, when the excitement of the honeymoon and travel was over, the inconveniences of his old age started to surface. Soon I noticed his old skin, his aged-cheese breath, his legs full of pink and purple veins that extended from his flesh and crept onto the bedsheet and up onto my pillow, up the sides of the bed. He would touch me just as I was about to fall asleep, always sneaking up on me, never with any foreplay or playful teasing or a sweet word. He was inept and boring—a businessman with no charm, no humour, no character, really . . . no personality . . . A man with no qualities . . . He insisted on taking me to church every Sunday to mingle with other merchants' wives. I was subjected to unrelenting boredom and disgust. We spent our lives going from one restaurant to another . . . Food and work were his existence. His joy was to meet a villager who could sell him fresh vegetables, or a fisherman who brought him a live catch wobbling and suffocating for lack of salt and sea. All he cared about was money, cars and food . . . Oh, the platitudes I endured . . . Boredom has always been undermining . . . But before I could leave him, I found out I was pregnant. By then we were fighting every day. Boredom had ruined me, and everything around me seemed dull and tasteless. When he sensed my dissatisfaction, he became jealous and abusive. I was trapped, with nowhere to go and no one to complain to but El-Marquis. By then my cousin was living the high life—he had a good teaching job, his inheritance had come through, and he made even more money by appropriating and translating Harlequin romances into Arabic under the pseudonym of Nuwas, as in the Arab poet Abu Nuwas. He made so much money from the sales of these romances. Saudi women bought his books by the thousands, and women from all over the Arab world would send him secret letters of admiration. We used to sit for hours and read them and laugh. Some of his readers would come to Lebanon and he would embezzle them, corrupt them, sleep with them. Saudi princesses, Moroccan royals . . . But the irony is that my life turned out to be just as ridiculous as one of his cheap novels.

I took a lover, of course I did—and how could I not? El-Marquis laughed about it. He teased me about the castle, the maids and the rich husband—the price to pay for a golden chain. He called me Bovary. He was the only one who knew about my lover. A woman always manages to have affairs, he would say. I was very pretty and loved life; I would walk into a room and all the men's heads would turn. My lover was a young major in the army who lived in the same building as us. He was handsome and smart. He read—and not just the newspapers, but books too, and he shared these with me. He gave me an education. He was sensitive and clever. We fell in love when we met in our building. His straight dark hair and uniform made me weep at night out of desire. We would meet in the garage, inside his car with its tinted windows. And we made love on weekdays for the next twenty years, right under the nose of my husband. I loved this man. I loved the way he wore his uniform, always tidy and pressed and clean. He smelled of French cologne, and he bought me books . . .

He loved me as well, I know he did. He never married out of his love for me. He was also involved in politics. Sometimes he would hint at top secret things, and once he said that he was in danger—and I cried. He said that the militia were after him. He died in a car accident, in the same car we made love in, on his way back from the regiment. He was speeding because another car with three armed men was chasing him, people said. His car flew off a ramp and landed on the street below. Luckily, it was early in the morning and there was no one on the road below . . . It's a comfort that he died without costing innocents their lives . . .

I couldn't attend the funeral because I was afraid to be seen in my devastation, and my husband would have asked me questions if he saw me crying over a neighbour. At a funeral, a neighbour's grief shouldn't outweigh the sadness and pain of the deceased's family—but I knew that mine would have, and people would wonder how I knew the dead soldier. I cried for weeks, alone and in secret. I cried for months at his apartment door. I would go to the bathroom and lock myself in and cry, or climb the stairs until I reached his door, hoping to hear his boots on the floor again . . . I never visited his grave until the death of my husband. I was afraid that my husband or one of his colleagues might follow me.

I would have written in my will that I don't want to be buried in the same place as my wretched husband—I was afraid of his decaying smell while he was alive; imagine it in death!—but I am afraid that my kids will insist on burying me with him regardless of my wishes. They have told me that my place is by his side. So, my dear Pavlov, here is my request. After my children bury me with my husband, I want you to steal my body—exhume it. And I want you to bury me with my lover. You will be notified of my death, and I will be grateful from beyond the grave. I have already arranged for one of my major's closest friends in the military to help us. And if there is a link here from the other side, I will make sure your life is filled with good fortune. And please, before you bury me with my lover, make sure that I have a smile on my face? Sprinkle some of this French perfume on me. Will you do this for me?

At this, the food arrived—and it was as excellent as Souad had promised. She and Pavlov, and Manneh and Hanneh, ate fish and drank beside the sea. When they were done, Souad kissed Pavlov on the forehead, and wept. Then she handed him an envelope of money and thanked him.

You will see me again, she said. Talkative or not, she added, and released Pavlov's hand.

MADAME AND MONSIEUR FIORA

Pavlov mostly kept to his bed for the next three days. He read. He left the house only to go to the grocery store for batteries for the flashlight, a few candles, cigarettes and ice. At night, the electricity went down. On the third morning, early, he was awakened by gun battles and bombs falling. Sirens and speeding cars came and went through the neighbourhood. He didn't need to listen to the news—war and its constant mayhem inevitably ended up parading itself beneath his window. Tales of combat deaths, sniper deaths, deaths by misadventure, old age, accidents, car crashes, massacres, drowning, collapsing houses, stillbirth, hunger and gluttony, execution, slaughter—all converged under his balcony.

The fourth day after his meeting with Souad, Pavlov ventured out to buy bread. He overheard the grocer talking about the death of a neighbour, Madame Fiora. She had been shot by her husband, the grocer said, but even though she was

RAWI HAGE ~ 144

the victim of this crime, the Church refused to bury her in the cemetery—because a Communist, an atheist such as her, he said, deserves only to be buried in hell.

Madame Fiora had been a tall Spaniard with broad shoulders, long gypsy-black hair, and wide eyes like those of an Arab, whose seductiveness she accentuated by lining the edges with thick black kohl. Two hand-drawn black lines substituted for her plucked eyebrows and formed permanent swords below her spacious forehead and above those big eyes. A grand madame with imposing breasts and strong shoulders, she had used the magnitude of her body to make her way among the diminutive local men. She wore thick high heels, which made her taller than anyone in the neighbourhood, man or woman. Her deep voice was vocal against all injustices, from the piling of garbage on the sidewalks to the whistles of men as young women passed by. She was a kind of Jeanne d'Arc, with enough broken Arabic to intimidate a nation of mustachioed men.

Her husband, Monsieur Fiora—as everyone called him in deference to his wife—was a small man, bald, who wore bureaucrat's glasses and a humble, defeated demeanour. He always carried a brown, soft leather briefcase. He hurried home each afternoon with an air of anxiety, but walked to work each morning with an air of relief, as if in respite from the antagonistic climate of his home. An accountant who had studied under French missionaries, he was meticulous, principled and studious, and took pride in his conventionality, honesty and obedience to institutions, secular or religious. On Sundays, he greeted everyone in his most proper manner, with a French Catholic *Bon dimanche!* He never left home without his tie or his well-polished shoes, and during the mild winter he could not be parted from his silk scarf, leather gloves and one-hundred-percent lambswool hat.

Lately, he had been seen with bruises on his face and a black eye, which he blamed on the unsafe sidewalks, on the startling effects of the falling bombs, which caused him to lose his footing, and on the lack of electricity that forced him to take the stairs with all their treacherous obstacles. In short, he blamed his bruises on the dysfunction of law and authority, and the presence of mayhem and chaos. But the neighbourhood joke was that Monsieur Fiora was a stickler for order, forever calling up the militia to report someone who honked his car horn at six in the morning or when the bulb on a traffic light had burned out. The thuggish members of the militia thought these were prank calls at first, but soon realized that they were dealing with a genuinely concerned citizen, which made their exchanges with him even funnier.

Madame Fiora was known for her closeness to other women—and it was true that some women in the neighbourhood loved her. Others looked at her as an arrogant giant with a deep disdain for religion and belief, an eccentric foreigner who shamelessly sent her husband to buy groceries while she lingered at home with her books. They resented her brusque manners, her intimidating aloofness when she disapproved of someone. Her two grown sons lived abroad. Their Spanish citizenship allowed them to travel freely all over the world, without the hassle of camping at the doors of embassies, begging for visas, as every Lebanese citizen endured during war. One of Madame Fiora's sons was a doctor, the other a photographer who spent his days in artistic circles, reading, drinking and smoking hash, weed, anything he could get his hands on.

Madame Fiora was a fierce atheist. Her contempt for religion was overt—and often offensive to her neighbours. After the outbreak of the war, as religious zealotry became fierce, her life had became more secluded. But in a basement shelter during the bombings, she had befriended a widow by the name of Janette Chalitta and become her most loving companion. She gave advice to Janette and, with her height and her strength and demeanour, protected her friend from men's belligerence, abuse, advances and sexual insinuations.

The surviving priest asked Monsieur Fiora about his wife's refusal to accompany him to church on Sundays, and he confessed that his wife did not believe in God, that she was a heathen. And then he disclosed that she frequently beat him up. He knelt in front of the priest and wept.

You must take control of the situation, the priest said. You are the man of the house. Do whatever you have to do. It's your house.

A few days later, Monsieur Fiora bought a gun from a militia kid. He went to Abou-Antoun's café, ate a bit of bread, some *labneh* and olives, and then he drank arak until a late hour. He walked home, opened the door, and before his wife had the chance to interrogate him about his drunkenness or where he had been, he pulled out the gun and aimed it at her. He pursued her through the house and shot her five times.

Madame Fiora was heard screaming for help, fleeing from one room to another. A neighbour banged on the door. Monsieur Fiora opened it with a Smith & Wesson in his hand.

It's over, he said.

The local militiamen were called to the crime scene. One of the thugs slapped Monsieur Fiora repeatedly. Then he was taken to militia headquarters and locked in a makeshift cell in the bathroom. His sons were informed of what had happened by telex, and both caught the next flight from Barcelona. They demanded to see their father. The militia refused them access, and informed them that their mother's body was in the morgue, awaiting burial. No one knew where to bury this unbeliever, this woman who had beaten her husband. At last, her widowed friend and lover, Janette Chalitta, pleaded with the clergy to allow Madame Fiora a proper burial, but they stalled, giving her convoluted excuses about the scarcity of lots, the backlog of dead. And then one of them hinted at Madame Fiora's overt atheism.

It was Pavlov who, that morning after leaving the grocer's, and out of respect for Madame Fiora's body, sought out the two sons. They were both staying in the family home. It had been cleaned of the blood of their mother who, while wounded during the chase, had crawled over carpets and under dining room chairs trying to escape her husband. When Pavlov knocked at the door of the house, he stood silent, calm, his eyes lowered, his hands joined in front of his stomach in a sign of reverence—an indication that he, the man who called himself Pavlov, did not possess the arrogance of the authorities nor the intrusiveness of the neighbours.

He introduced himself as an undertaker and the son of an undertaker, and asked if he could come in.

The sons stepped aside to let him in, curious.

Once seated in the living room, Pavlov asked if they had decided yet on a burial.

The sons confirmed that the Church was blocking them from using the cemetery.

Were they open to the possibility of privately cremating their mother's body? asked Pavlov.

The son who was a doctor was reluctant, suspicious. But the bohemian son was open to the idea—even excited by it. A long discussion ensued, over drinks, on the merits of fire versus earth. The Bohemian became drunk and agitated, and went on a philosophical rant about the futility of religious rituals. He insisted that his mother was an atheist, and that in one of their phone conversations she had told him she didn't care how her body was disposed of after her death. The doctor dismissed his brother's arguments, accusing him of lying. But finally he accepted Pavlov's proposal—on condition that he could witness the burning of the body himself to make sure that he received their mother's ashes and not those of an imposter or a dog—or a goat, for that matter.

Pavlov informed the brothers that all would be done with the utmost discretion. In any case, he said, the location of the crematorium was kept secret because of the threat of violence and retaliation from an underground society of dangerous people.

At this, they shook hands and agreed on a plan.

Following Pavlov's instructions, the doctor withdrew a

large sum of money and went to meet the head of the neigh-bourhood militia. After that, he met the local priest, paid him handsomely, and received his mother's death certificate and authorization for repossession of the body. The sons declared solemnly that their mother would be shipped back to Spain, to be buried in the Basque country of her birth.

Meanwhile, the Bohemian found a dealer, a thug by the name of Faddoul, who sold him some hash, and who owed a debt to Pavlov, because Pavlov's father had buried his parents and Faddoul had never paid up.

A couple of nights later, Pavlov acquired Madame Fiora's body from the hospital morgue and drove up into the moun-tains, with the two brothers following in their father's car. It was past midnight and the roads were unlit. The brothers were unfamiliar with the terrain but managed to follow the trail of the deathmobile's lights. When the little convoy arrived at the house in the mountains, the three men carried the body inside. The doctor asked to examine the body to make sure it was their mother's, and the Bohemian asked to be given time to roll a joint and smoke it before the bag was unzipped.

Pavlov nodded, and the three of them went outside and stood by the door. The Bohemian offered the doctor a puff, but his brother refused. Pavlov took the cigarette and inhaled, his eyes shut, then exhaled and extended his arm to pass it back. He went to the kitchen, searched for alcohol in the cupboard, and brought back three glasses and what remained of the bottle of whisky. They drank. The doctor poured a second round, then they all retuned to the house to face the dead mother.

Pavlov delicately unzipped the bag. Madame Fiora was naked inside it. Her breasts were falling sideways over her arms, and her face had the severe expression of someone who had seen death marching towards her.

Pavlov could tell from their faces how the dead had encountered their end. There were those who looked surprised, their necks curved like a question mark; there were those who wore expressions of nonchalance, judging by the relaxed pose of their hands; there were others who had anticipated their long-awaited ending, and had impassive faces of boredom, perhaps even relief. Those who were murdered looked stunned—unlike the suicides, whose faces carried the angst of the universe, overwhelmed yet defiant in a fuck-you-all farewell. The lucky ones were those who died peacefully in their sleep, their faces serene and calm.

After the opening of the bag, there was silence. The doctor mumbled the name of his father two or three times in anger. The Bohemian glanced at his mother, said, It's her, and zipped up the bag again.

Pavlov opened the furnace door. Together, they all slid the body inside. Pavlov released the gas and ignited the fire. Light flickered over the brothers' faces. When the bag caught fire, Pavlov closed the door and walked away, leaving the sons in the presence of their burning mother.

The rumour was that Monsieur Fiora escaped custody during the re-enactment of his wife's murder. The man who murdered his wife had escaped! The official account was that, on the way back to militia headquarters after the re-enactment of the crime, bombs started to fall. The fighters found cover inside a building, and that was when Monsieur Fiora took flight.

In the re-enactment, the police had asked him to walk down the road as if coming home from Abou-Antoun's restaurant on the evening of the crime. They had handed him the little leather briefcase he always carried, containing his personal documents and his gloves. They had even made him wear his one-hundred-percent lambswool hat, the one he had worn for thirty-five years, and which Madame Fiora's father had given him once upon a time in Spain. It was surprising that his father-in-law had given him a hat at all. When Monsieur Fiora had first encountered the man, his future father-in-law had been furious. His daughter had brought home a Moor! He wouldn't look Monsieur Fiora in the eye. He told his daughter that he detested the Moors because they had fought as mercenaries with Franco. But then one day this very man had walked up to Monsieur Fiora and hugged him and given him the hat. Then he had said, Now I know you're not a Moor.

Yes, Monsieur Fiora had escaped—the militia admitted this. He had escaped because of the falling bombs! But the truth was that Monsieur Fiora was handed over to his sons by the head of the local militia, who had arranged for the farcical re-enactment of the crime after the sons bribed the men in charge.

After being handed over, Monsieur Fiora spent the night at Pavlov's, in Pavlov's parents' room. That evening, the doctor entered the room where his father was sleeping, and through

the door Pavlov could hear him shouting at his father. Meanwhile, the Bohemian smoked in the living room. Then the
doctor stormed out of the house and his brother followed.

Late that night, Monsieur Fiora knocked at Pavlov's door.
He asked if he could have a cigarette and something to drink.
Pavlov went to the kitchen and found a bottle of arak. He
poured himself a glass and offered one to Monsieur Fiora. They
smoked and drank and sat quietly.

After a few rounds, Monsieur Fiora asked, What is your
name?

Call me Pavlov.

Well, Pavlov, my sons made me sign my will, leaving them
everything, the house, the money in the bank, everything,
Monsieur Fiora said. My wife wanted me dead and now my
sons want me dead. I am dead. He started to cry uncontrollably.

Pavlov refilled the old man's glass and went back to his
own room, leaving his guest alone and crying, in a house
that over the years had witnessed the fall of many tears.

The two sons showed up early the next morning. Pavlov had
a coffin ready, with a bottle of water inside and some food.
Monsieur Fiora was put inside it, and instructed not to move
or make a sound. Consider yourself a mummy, his doctor son
said. Pavlov and the sons drove to the port, and handed the
casket over to a shipping agent along with the death papers of
Madame Fiora and the permit to repatriate a cadaver. At each
step along the way, someone was given a bribe: the agent, the

port officials, the boat's captain. It was agreed between the sons that the doctor would accompany the coffin on its journey.

Once they passed into the open sea, two sailors witnessed the opening of the coffin on the deck. Terrified, one shouted and crossed himself while the other held a rigging knife. Identify yourself! he demanded of Monsieur Fiora. Right on cue, the captain showed up and calmed the sailors down. Both started to laugh—and then the younger sailor laughed for such a long time, he became hysterical and his laughter hit the waves and skimmed the water and hovered and stayed there for a while before it abruptly stopped. Monsieur Fiora stood up, climbed out of the coffin and breathed the fresh air. He smiled as he held the railing and looked at the horizon.

After a moment, he entered the cabin and asked for some water. He drank this, then walked out on the deck again. His wool hat was on his head and he folded it over his ears. His son provided him with a jacket, in a gesture that made him cry.

A few hours later, the doctor released his mother's ashes over the sea while his father wept on deck.

The next morning, the father was nowhere to be seen. The captain and his sailors searched high and low, but Monsieur Fiora had vanished.

The doctor stood out on the deck and told the captain that his father must have thrown himself overboard. A suicide. He studied the horizon and smoked until the ship arrived in Spain.

THE HYENA IS IN HEAT

One day, as Pavlov stood at his window above the road, he imagined Rex the dog looking his way. That night, he dreamed of the dog barking at him, and a few days later he thought he saw Rex at his door. As he opened his door, he saw the shadow of a dog rushing up the stairs to settle on the balcony. So Pavlov joined Rex there.

Man and dog heard moaning coming from the cemetery. The hyena is in heat, Pavlov whispered to Rex, and her fighter is thrusting between her thighs. Dog and man listened to his cousin's mating cries, and even sniffed the air for wetness and heat. He could picture his cousin with her palms flat on the ground, above the buried skeletons and the sharp pebbles that wild animals endure when the weight of their body presses on their paws.

He walked to the fridge, still thinking of his cousin's knees sweating above the burial ground.

And there they are, he said to the ghost dog. There they are, the hyena and Son of Mechanic. Fucking in the domain of the dead, oblivious to all those who have passed, all those who existed, all who once gorged and defecated and are now devoured by vermin and mud.

It must thrill the mechanic's son, Pavlov continued. He must be bewitched by this little laughing daughter of death. Attractions reveal our deepest love for violence, as you know. This mechanic's son is surely enchanted by the idea of the gravedigger's daughter offering him her thighs. Look at him! Swinging his testicles like holy incense above the altar of the dead, his hands pulling and pushing her hips back and forth to the cycle of moons and ocean tides, panting heavily like Marathon, that famous Athenian, racing towards his own death to deliver news of victory. And I have good news for *you*, my dear Rex: he is stretching her back and forth as if rolling out dough, with equal parts love and repulsion, fucking back and forth with the retreat velocity of a cranking gun, ejaculating onto the fecund earth, to fertilize the skulls of the dead and lubricate their moistureless organs . . .

A humorous couple, Pavlov said.

And the dog repeated, A humorous couple indeed.

I have never witnessed such an act of transgression against death, he said to the dog. Have you?

The dog shook his head.

Yes, fucking at the graves of all those dead people who are no longer capable of seducing, moaning and caressing. Or maybe fucking in memory of those who once seduced, moaned and caressed? A heroic act, then, I hear you say. One that transcends all the tears, music, pain and agony, which for years has paraded past our window.

Well, indeed, this heathen fucking is beautiful, Pavlov leaned in to whisper in Rex's ghost ear. This animalistic urge that overcomes all rituals, respect and ancestral worship is perhaps the most truthful act of both of our species. I tell you, Rex—and I hope you will not feel betrayed by what I am about to say—in this moment of esteem and admiration, I regret slapping my cousin in the face that day. She is, after all, the product of a long lineage that turned our road into an arcade for the procession of coffins, and a passageway between existence and extinction.

Maybe, Pavlov declared to the halo above Rex's head, my cousin is no longer satisfied with witnessing death. Maybe she aspires to join the immortals such as Hera or Athena. Maybe she seeks to elevate herself and become a flesh-loving Goddess, with offerings buried at her feet and under her soft, fertile belly, her fingers open against the ground and beckoning in the direction of the abyss and ecstasy. What courage, what beauty and truth! An act of future reproduction above past decay. The immediacy, the proximity of the cycle of birth and death have never been as united as they are in this moment. And what, my dear Rex, could be more comforting and truthful than contemplating fucking near all these decaying remains? Oh, the brilliance of it all. Unification, unification . . .

Furthermore, the dog pointed out, there's no difference between death and birth if one apprehends them with the same joyful intensity of wagging tails.

The little girl I remember, with snot falling from her nose, often in tears and dirty clothes, has asked her lover to turn me into an offering, Pavlov whispered in admiration. An offering to bribe the gods. And why not? he proclaimed to the dog. We all sacrifice something in our relentless quest for deification! It has always been an exchange. And what exchange doesn't entail a loss or a sacrifice?

Or a cross, the dog said, and smiled. Then added: Apotheosis! A human obsession, and a disease.

Pavlov nodded thoughtfully. Yes, Rex, well said. The very same word came to my mind. My cousin was seeking her own apotheosis. A sacrifice in order to bribe the council of the gods. So the hyena sent her Helot, that fighter, to kill me at my window. She wanted a human offering, but in the end she settled for a dog as a sacrifice.

Which reminds me to pour some ice on your headless remains. Stay! Pavlov ordered the dog. Do not move. And stop shivering.

WATCHING

The next morning, Pavlov knocked at the door of the house where the Bohemian was staying. He paced as he waited for the door to open.

The Bohemian let him in. They both sat in silence for a while, until at last the Bohemian handed Pavlov money for his services. The Bohemian looked sickly, Pavlov noticed. He was skinny, belonging to that breed of men who, due to their nocturnal habits, ruinous existence, drinking and chain-smoking, never gain weight. Pavlov knew this kind well: self-haters at permanent war with themselves until death comes to solve their irreconcilable differences. Their long monologues were sometimes prophetic and substantive—at the same time, they were all too aware of their minuscule role in the cosmic comedy and their inescapably low status. But they had neither the strength nor the will to repair whatever was broken in them. They tended to be pathetic huggers and ferocious kissers, and their laughter was followed by a long fit of coughing and spitting. Nudity in all seasons was a must. They welcomed you into their homes in their underwear, or an open shirt and unbuckled pants. Everything in their world stayed open—their windows, their smoking nostrils, their toe-revealing slippers; they were the enemies of curtains, shut bathroom doors, closed closets.

They are a type, Pavlov imagined, men whose birth marks a futile beginning and for whom death is no grand ending but the final small act in a long march to the always-open casket. They are forever outside paradise, in life or in death. They are open books who feel their only redemption might be in every-thing else remaining open too, and everything openly said.

Pavlov asked to borrow the Bohemian's car, which had belonged to Monsieur Fiora and had not yet been sold. When the Bohemian asked why, Pavlov replied that he wanted to watch someone from afar, and that his own hearse was con-spicuous. The Bohemian was hesitant but intrigued. He moved closer to Pavlov, offered him hash and asked if he had heard about his father's disappearance.

Pavlov shook his head.

The Bohemian handed Pavlov the keys to the little Fiat.

Pavlov drove through the neighbourhood and parked near Son of Mechanic's house. He sat low, only his eyes and the top of his head visible above the steering wheel, and heard himself say, Oh, oh, look who's coming, Son of Mechanic is on his way! Then the chorus in Pavlov's head sang, Now he's opening the trunk of his car! Now he is changing his jacket, and now he is pulling out his Russian Kalashnikov—how Orthodox of him. He's looking for his car keys, opening the front door and getting into his seat . . . Getting into his seat, the chorus intoned, getting into his seat . . .

And Son of Mechanic's car moved off along the road, heading out of the neighbourhood and away from his lover and her bed of stones and crosses. Pavlov waited, and when Son of Mechanic had passed the olive tree in the distance, Pavlov followed behind in the Fiat that had belonged to Monsieur Fiora. He tracked the car through empty roads until Son of Mechanic arrived at the local militia headquarters.

He watched Son of Mechanic park, get out and climb into a jeep with three other fighters. He followed the jeep along the highway towards the port then up into downtown, until it came to a stop near the Green Line. This was where the heaviest fighting occurred between the opposing factions. Pavlov continued past in his little car, then parked under a nearby bridge and got out. He entered a building that looked out over the Green Line, and climbed the stairs to the top floor. The building had been bombed, and its remaining walls were pitted with bullet holes. It smelled of moist cement, and the stairs were littered with broken glass and chunks of concrete. Human feces dotted the hallway.

So this is where these war heroes defecate: between the walls of their bombarded city. And how interesting that they do defecate, after all, Pavlov reminded himself. Only Byzantine angels do not defecate! Although even that is debatable.

He found a spot at a window and watched his foe, the mechanic's son. The kid was sitting on a plastic chair beside his fellow soldiers. He was acting silly, like a child playing, walking around and making grand gestures, and occasionally wrestling with his companions. He had shed his role as a lover, fighter and killer, and metamorphosed into a jester. Pavlov frowned. Jesters may have some wisdom, but they are also meek and gutless, cowardly buffoons, he thought. And this one hid behind the shipping containers filled with sand that split the city of Beirut into two separate oceans.

By noon, the fighters seemed infected by sleepiness and inertia. They lounged on their plastic chairs, and even lay down on a mattress in the shade of a building, as they waited for the killing to start again. All was calm and Pavlov watched in vengeful silence, gazing out at the empty streets and the grass that grew everywhere. After watching for hours, he walked back to the Fiat and drove home. There he stood at his window and looked down along the road of death. Those fighters were bound to pass by one day, he predicted. It was boredom that would kill them.

He was reminded of his own solitude, and decided to drive the little car back to the Bohemian. The bombs had started to fall again—they whizzed above the Fiat and landed with a familiar sound, that of metal dropped on roofs and empty water tanks. It was like the muffled sound of titanic collisions underwater, metal against metal, the sound of violence made by a two-legged species of alchemists who managed to mix earth with fire and solidify lava into glittering swords, javelins and nails for crucifixions. Oh, the shining armour of this species that only ceased to glitter when dipped in blood. Pavlov's father had once informed him that Orthodox Jews never put metal in their coffins—except perhaps for the lead fillings in a cadaver's teeth. The burial was purely of wood, because maybe, just maybe, the presence of metal inside a coffin would stop it from floating when the grand flood comes again. The sea, Pavlov had imagined as a kid, would one day be filled with wooden coffins floating on salty water—millions of little boats resurrected from beneath the waves to surge above the flood water. What a sight! Thousands upon thousands of resurrected bones paddling with wooden oars towards a promised paradise. Pavlov laughed as he drove in circles, looking for a parking space on the Bohemian's street. We poor, silly humans, he thought, and the stories we tell ourselves.

Finally, Pavlov found a spot where the Fiat would fit, although it blocked a large car. But who would want to leave and drive now under the falling bombs? He went up to the Bohemian's apartment on the fifth floor, and on the way passed families taking shelter in the stairwell, kids playing cards, mothers nervously assessing the proximity of the falling bombs with the expertise of military personnel. He saluted everyone as he climbed the steps.

The door to the apartment was open. The Bohemian was standing on his balcony, pointing his camera at the sky. When Pavlov entered, he glanced back for a second then invited him to have a seat.

Do you know why it's possible to take a photograph of a falling bomb in Beirut and not elsewhere? he asked Pavlov.

Pavlov stayed silent.

Because of the sun, the Bohemian said. The plentiful light allows us to shoot at a high shutter speed. A high shutter speed freezes passing, flying, speeding objects in a photograph. Just a technical observation. This is not always possible in an overcast climate. Taking images of descending bombs is more feasible in sunny places, and in this century there have been more falling bombs in sunny places than in northern overcast places. He laughed.

Pavlov ignored this, and reached for a cigarette. He placed the car keys on the table and was turning to leave when the Bohemian called him back.

Where did you go? he asked.

To the Green Line.

Did you reach the fighting?

Pavlov nodded.

Next time, I am coming with you. What better place to get an image of a falling bomb than from the battlefield itself?

Pavlov turned again to leave.

The car is yours anytime, the Bohemian declared, and clicked the camera shutter, pointing it at Pavlov.

⚓

Later, in front of his own window, Pavlov watched the twilight burial of an old man. Three old women walked behind the coffin, and only Pavlov's brute uncles and their son were present to carry the casket to the gate. The three old women with their faces covered in black lace veils walked in complete silence, their backs curved, their shoes round, their dresses covering their knees and frail bodies, their feet advancing in careful movements, barely leaving the crust of the ground.

The priest seemed in a hurry to get it over with. Pavlov could tell from the economical swinging of incense and the unenthusiastic, disingenuous mumble of his prayers. His expression was irritated, his backward glances at the slowness of the mourners scornful. Yes, he was in a hurry to get it done but the old women were slowing his pace. The priest repeated the same refrain, Your slave, Joseph Knefeh, have mercy on him—nothing too musical, loud or elaborate. This must be a low-grade, basic-package burial, or maybe the priest was doing it for free.

Pavlov watched as his uncles struggled to carry the cheap coffin, the idiotic son of the younger uncle barely tall enough to help. Eventually he went downstairs to assume once more his old role of pallbearer. He took the front handle and walked as his uncle Mounir, right behind him, whispered threats about the hearse in his ear. Together, they reached the hole in the ground. The interment was done in a rush; the prayers were brief. The three old women did not cry.

The man in the coffin had died alone, and the three women were only his neighbours. He had lived too long—outliving all his children, even his twin grandsons who had both died carrying weapons in the war. Hearing the family name of the deceased, Pavlov remembered the burial of the grandsons in the early days of the war. Their two coffins had danced and swayed in sync to the music of the band. The Knefeh twins had died in the same battle, or so went the official story. The truth was that they were killed by their peers. They and two other militiamen had managed to secure a jewellery district downtown, and had gone straightaway to the safe of an Armenian jeweller and blown it up. The brothers were carrying off the spoils in bags when they were promptly gunned down in the street by their two accomplices. These accomplices were hard-asses, feared in the neighbourhood, criminals who had moved quickly up the ranks in the militia hierarchy. They were executioners, racketeers and gamblers who drove fancy cars and did contract killings to secure stolen merchandise from the commercial district. Always on cocaine, they were psychopaths to be avoided at all costs. The rule was: never look them in the eye or get in a fight with them over a parking space or challenge them to a car race. They would kill without a blink, then go eat at their favourite joint. One of them had a poked-out eye. In his youth before the war, he had been in a fight and been hit so hard that his left eye popped out of its socket. He had carried it in his palm as he ran all the way to the hospital. Pavlov remembered seeing the two killers carrying the twin brothers' coffins at the procession, wearing Ray-Bans that hid their vacant eyes. The whole neighbourhood had known they were the killers, yet these assassins had continued down the road, dancing with the coffins, gold chains ornamenting their butchers' necks, gold rings glittering in the summer sun.

That autumn, the father of the twins had died of heartbreak, and then the mother fell into a deep and final slumber.

And now the grandfather too had died, and no one was left to carry his coffin except for the family of undertakers. And no one was left to walk behind that coffin but three old women who quietly, timidly, beneath the black veils covering their transitory old faces, mourned the end of a lineage and the inevitability of extinction.

SEX AND DEATH

Early the next morning, Pavlov heard an assertive knock at his door. He anticipated the return of his brute uncles, their bulging bellies presenting themselves on behalf of everything and everyone. It was their bellies that expressed their state of mind, their vision in life, their convictions and causes—including their persistent demands for possession of Pavlov's hearse. They were driven by the needs of their bellies to expand and conquer. In contrast to Pavlov's father, who had been slim and energetic, the brothers loved sloth. It was the fruit of their labour, which they equated with good morality, responsibility, provision and success. They moved slowly, and their slowness was determined and menacing. With their high chests with saggy breasts, and the fat under their arms that pushed their limbs outwards, they fancied themselves righteous knights in shining armour, and owners of the castle next door.

They banged on the door as if with the intention of breaking it and gathering its wood to use as joints in Pavlov's coffin. Their utilitarian tendencies were impressive, Pavlov admitted. His uncles were scavengers who recycled and buried everything. At the sound of yet more knocks, he hunched his back like the conditioned animal he was, inclined his ear towards the noise and reached for his rifle.

He carried his rifle downstairs, laid it against the wall and opened the door. And as he opened it, Rex's shadow escaped, running towards the gate of the cemetery and releasing a long, sad howl.

It wasn't the brute uncles at his door after all; it was the Bohemian, drunk and high. He smiled at the sight of Pavlov and, without waiting for an invitation, entered the house and stood at the bottom of the stairs laughing. He bent down to study the arabesque motif of the tiles on the floor. Pavlov went back upstairs and the Bohemian followed, barely functional, still lucid but visibly intoxicated. He dragged his open sandals up each stair, placing each foot with difficulty, lifting his soles with effort. The earth, the gods, the devils—all beings that dwelled over and under the earth—pulled him down, making him step with the heaviness of the damned whose souls inevitably give way to gravity. His entrails had absorbed a high level of alcohol, and his body appeared wet, and he radiated the pungent smell of cigarettes, thick and permanent, trailed by a hazy vapour and mumbling and curses. He reached the top of the staircase, where he threw his weight on Pavlov, showering him with drool and mumbled words and kisses. Then he detached himself and collapsed on the sofa. He declared: I need to get that photograph. A photograph of a bomb falling would be priceless.

Pavlov went to the kitchen and boiled water to prepare coffee. Through the door, he could hear the Bohemian talking about settling in Beirut and never returning to Spain, claiming that the only meaningful experience was the constant threat of death and living through war made him feel alive. The only way to escape this miserable eternal condition is through the courage to position oneself in proximity to danger, even death! he shouted. His loud voice disturbed Pavlov, but soon the Bohemian started to sway and hum a tune in a low voice. Pavlov, watching from the kitchen, was pleased to see the Bohemian dance between his empty walls and over the tiles of his home.

Listen, Pavlov, the Bohemian shouted again. Listen to this drunk man, because even those who are not all there, if you know what I mean, have something to contribute. Wisdom doesn't require full consciousness. Listen, the fatal mistake is to forbid the intoxication of the body. Sex, its corporeal intoxication, is short-lived—in this world at least. But substances can be a lifelong project, as long as nature provides. Look at my mother, for instance . . . She disdained sex. But now that my mother is gone, I have every reason to stay in this land. I couldn't have possibly lived with her nearby. In a way, her death is a relief, liberating, the passing story of a human creature who existed, interacted, reacted, but did nothing too special, nothing worth mentioning or memorable. Stories are told, dear Pavlov, but are not remembered forever. Someday, no one will want to tell them anymore. No one will be left to tell them. But what an ending my mother had. What a grand ending! She never approved of my life, nor I of hers for that matter. She only admired my brother, the doctor. She worshipped the doctor. The problem with my parents was that they never came to terms with their own sexuality, he said, and smirked. They were both latent homosexuals, like much of humanity, and they never came to terms with it. Whatever that widow woman who befriended my mother might say . . . Are you a homosexual, Pavlov? Are you? Answer me, my man, are you?

Pavlov stood in the middle of the room, a tray in his hand bearing two small coffee cups and a coffee pot, and ignored the question. The Bohemian, Pavlov noticed, looked awful—not only drunk but dirty, neglected, wearing mismatched clothes. He recalled his own father's delicate attention to details and appearances—the makeup he had applied to the dead, his suave manner around the cadavers, his choice of shoes for them, how he had combed their hair. Disguise before dust, his father used to sing in his low voice, wearing his long apron, even occasionally clapping his hands and furtively dancing around the coffins.

How about you, Pavlov? the Bohemian rambled. Were your parents homosexuals, deviants, transgressors, filthy sinners? Hahaha, do tell. You're a handsome fellow, Pavlov. With your curly, wild hair and your broad, strong shoulders. You should go to Europe, you'll have so much success. Some women, or men, whatever your preference, would fuck you just for the colour of your skin and the look in your eyes. But tell me, Pavlov, how do you feel about death? Does it excite you? Does the idea of death ever give you an erection? You're a lucky man, Pavlov. You like these endings because they assure you of your own existence. The end can only be witnessed by those who persevere, the quiet survivors. Death can't be experienced by the dead, unless you're immortal like a god. Are you immortal, Pavlov? Are you an ending that never ends?

The Bohemian began to roll some hash. He shouted, Let's smoke! And he lit up, inhaling and, after a moment, exhaling with a long sigh. What I need from you, Pavlov, is an introduction. I know that you went to the Green Line the other day. I need you to take me there. You can use my father's car, but I need to get downtown so that I can take portraits of fighters. I am planning a series for a magazine. Maybe an exhibition one day. Art, baby, art!

Pavlov extended his hand. Give me the car keys, he said. He drank his last sip of coffee, told the Bohemian to finish his cup, and then they both went downstairs and got into the Fiat. Pavlov drove towards the centre of the city. The Bohemian smoked hash in the car, and Pavlov, liking the smell, smoked too.

Upon reaching the outskirts of downtown, Pavlov parked the car and he and the Bohemian entered the bombed building opposite Son of Mechanic's military unit. They both stood for a few minutes at the window Pavlov had found before, observing the empty plastic chairs in front of the shipping containers. Then the Bohemian turned away, told Pavlov not to wait and rushed back down the stairs.

Pavlov watched him crossing the street and walking towards the containers. The Bohemian carried a bag at his waist, his long hair reached his shoulders, and he wore a psychedelic tie-dyed shirt and hippy sandals that gave utmost liberty to his untrimmed nails and dirty toes. Once he arrived at the containers, he shouted and waved, and Son of Mechanic and another militia boy came out from behind the building, rifles in hand. They looked stunned and intrigued. Son of Mechanic wore a black T-shirt and the other kid was bare-chested, his hair wet and his face covered in shaving soap. The kid with soap on his face aimed his rifle at this man who had appeared from nowhere. The Bohemian raised his hands and continued shouting. Neither of the fighters seemed to be alarmed—cautious, but not alarmed. The Bohemian pointed at his bag. Gently, he put it on the ground, knelt down and opened it slowly. He pulled the camera out and started to gesticulate. There was an exchange that Pavlov couldn't hear. A few minutes later, the Bohemian was dancing in triumph and the fighters were laughing.

The Bohemian pointed his camera, and the fighters pointed their rifles vertically into the air, rested their arms on each other's shoulders and posed. The Bohemian clicked away, and then he laid the camera down and pulled out some cigarettes, offering them. He pulled out a bottle of whisky from the bag, and shared that too. But when he pointed towards the building where Pavlov was concealed, Pavlov decided to leave. He walked calmly towards the car, got in and drove home.

Pavlov found Hanneh and Manneh waiting at his door. They had come to inform him of the death of Souad, the woman he had met at the beach.

Pavlov asked for the location of the cemetery where Souad was buried. He would arrange the exhumation, he said, and they should return in two days, at midnight. Hanneh and Manneh nodded. They would inform their accomplice, the friend of the dead major who had been Souad's lover.

Two nights later, when the burial road beneath Pavlov's window was deserted, Hanneh and Manneh returned on their motorcycles. They followed Pavlov in his hearse to a coastal town. Over the gentle hills they drove, and through rows of pines with slim, elegant trunks, crooked and bashful in brown livery that opened into umbrella-like greenery on top. This small forest of pine stood watch over the road in a regiment of vertical wood lines, its high-arching boughs covering the blue sky. Finally the convoy arrived at a small cemetery. A man stood waiting at the gate: an undertaker named Gerious who wore long rubber boots and muddy khaki pants, shovel in hand. Together, they walked between the headstones, following the gravedigger's light, which shone along the ground, reviving a few names and illuminating a few beginnings and ends. In the daytime, Pavlov knew, there was a remarkable view from the graveyard of the horizon and the sea. In a place of such beauty, he thought, coffins should be hung high, suspended to face the water and pine trees and the ancient sky. I would dare to suspend them all, like branches bearing fruit. What a vision that would be for us all of what is to come, like the view of a sea storm to a seafarer watching from the shoreline.

They reached Souad's plot. In the hole, two ropes had already been laid around and under the coffin. All four men grabbed an end and raised the coffin to the surface. They laid it on the ground and caught their breath, then carried it to the deathmobile. Pavlov withdrew a stack of notes from his pocket and handed them to the gravedigger, who counted them and started to politely complain, reminding Pavlov of the risk he had taken and the sin he had committed towards the saints and his God. He had even opened the casket as instructed . . . Hell, he said. And he repeated, Hell! And in the name of the saints . . .

Pavlov proffered more cash, and the gravedigger was pleased. He shook Pavlov's hand, then returned to the hole in the ground. He swung his shovel, filling in the vacant space below.

Now let's find the colonel, Manneh said.

Pavlov and his companions drove back to the city. The two motorcycles rode ahead of the deathmobile this time, two escorts, two single lights shining on the road, ephemeral but continuous, inconspicuous yet visible, flitting along the lines of the earth with its abundance of vermin and flies. In time, they arrived at a military base, and a guard appeared. He seemed to be expecting them. He opened the gate and, without a word, directed them towards a jeep nearby. In front of it, a man in regimental uniform stood stoically.

Hanneh and Manneh got down from their motorcycles and went to meet the colonel. Pavlov stayed with Souad's body, noticing how the coffin's residue of earth had left its traces and fresh, moist smells of mud in the car. He opened the casket and perfumed Souad as she had requested, then placed the bottle in her hands and closed the lid.

The officer gestured for Pavlov to follow him in the hearse. The jeep continued to the edge of the military complex and out another gate. In their small convoy, they turned up the road and reached another gate. Four soldiers approached the deathmobile. They slid the coffin out, carried it to the end of the lot and disappeared behind another building.

We'll handle it from here, the officer said. Your mission is done. You're dismissed. He turned and walked away.

Hanneh and Manneh returned home with Pavlov. Upstairs in his apartment, they removed their leather jackets, their helmets and motorcycle leathers. They showered, and then slowly changed into their more feminine selves. They slipped on dresses, and made up their faces with puffs and brushes. Over the course of an hour, they went back and forth between the mirrors in the house, and finally they both slipped on high heels and stood before Pavlov.

So, they asked, what do you think?

Pavlov simply smiled and nodded.

They reached for their purses, pulled out envelopes of cash and handed them to him. Here is your share from beyond the grave.

As they turned to leave, Pavlov heard the loud shouts of the Bohemian below his window. He went downstairs with Hanneh and Manneh and opened the front door.

The encounter between the drunk photographer and the ladies ignited immediately with sparks and flirtations. Pavlov stood watching as the batting of eyelashes fanned flames. He witnessed a parade of little steps and twirled circles and minuscule turns, followed by seductive laughs, complimentary words and the holding of loose hands.

He saw, too, that the Bohemian was very excited at the sight of the girls, calling them lovely ladies, making Hanneh turn gracefully as he whistled sweet Spanish tunes. Hanneh and Manneh paused, then went back upstairs, followed by the Bohemian. They had decided to stay a while longer.

Eventually Pavlov went to bed, but long into the night he could hear the Bohemian's loud singing, his drunken monologues, and the women's joyful responses as they poured drinks and the bombs started to fall again. Quiet alternated with muffled screams, followed by more laughing and giggling and clinking of glasses, and that was when Pavlov fell into a deep sleep, and he dreamed of bells and he dreamed of the creature of death roaming the streets, reaching inside doors and windows, swinging his long cane. And he dreamed of an army of workers in assembly lines building wooden coffins and gravestones, standing in long rows, reciting the alphabet with hammers in their hands, and peddlers carrying black dresses and screaming, Sale, everything must go! And he saw headless dogs in heat fucking each other in long chains, and flashes of the decapitated priest trotting around performing obscene acts of anilingus and slurping and drinking from a golden cup, and he heard his mother's screams, and saw his father dancing with makeup brushes and bowties in his hands, and a grotesque woman opening a coffin in the middle of a wedding dance, and then the creature of death came towards him again and his stick shone—but Rex rushed to meet the creature and drowned him with his saliva, and Pavlov saw the Lady of the Stairs surfing above the grand wave of sputum, her feet moist and her hair long and flowing . . .

Loud laughter erupted from the living room and Pavlov woke in a sweat. He opened his eyes. He thought about the night's bombing and the new day's inevitable spectacle—the repeated parades of wailing beneath his window. And he thought about how, throughout the fall, the roads would flow, like schools of fish beneath the sea, with accumulated tears and surfing wooden boxes. And for the first time since the departure of the Lady of the Stairs, he thought about the weight of her little brother in his arms, and how he had washed her naked body. Departure is death, he thought, but death is inconsequential for those who have departed. Remembering her last glance towards his window made him want to weep, and he wondered if he would ever see her again. After she had left, he had searched for and found her name and address. He had, on one occasion, walked up the stairs to her family's apartment, and had even knocked at the door. There were crosses, flowers and icons leaning against it. The neighbours had come out and said to him, No one is there, everyone has gone. The whole family was killed. Weeded out. We built this shrine for them, they said, and we lit candles for them, but they are all gone, even the little boy. The family is extinct.

Pavlov woke again from his reverie, dismissed his macabre thoughts, walked to the bathroom and washed his face.

Only then did he notice the smell of cigarette smoke, alcohol and drugs—and suddenly remember the previous night.

He rushed into the living room and found clothing scattered on the sofa and on the floor. He followed the trail into the bedroom that his parents had once occupied and saw two beds filled with naked bodies. The Bohemian was sleeping in the arms of one of the ladies—Pavlov couldn't distinguish which—and his mother's separate bed had a single naked body in it, sound asleep. The room smelled of sex, cigarettes, alcohol and hash. There were traces of blood on the sheets, and the sheets had many wrinkles. Everything in the room was soiled and creased, and the three guests looked like a still photograph from the aftermath of a massacre, or a Roman orgy.

Pavlov closed the door and returned to the kitchen, where he opened the freezer and greeted the remains of his dog. He made coffee and lit a cigarette in preparation for the first parade.

While Hanneh and Manneh still slept, the Bohemian wandered out to stand next to Pavlov at the window. Pavlov offered a puff of his cigarette.

A coffin was passing below. It was a silent procession that could be seen but not heard.

These few left-over Christians in the Middle East should leave, the Bohemian said.

And go where? Pavlov asked.

They should leave this land and spread out all over the earth. The world is vast and these early converts are holding on, in vain, to their mythologies, religion, and a handful of picturesque valleys and mountains. Who and what are they fighting for? They should leave. Leave this country to the Muslims, and then the Muslims will leave it to someone else one day. I have never understood attachments to land and culture. Look at them, sliding one coffin after another into the pit! They wasted the little life they could have had elsewhere. They were never tolerated, and they tolerated no one. The Gods of these lands are cruel, jealous, petty and archaic. These converts should leave and roam the planet . . .

Then why are *you* still here? Pavlov asked.

The Bohemian laughed, meanly. Then he coughed, paused, looked Pavlov in the eye and said, I came to witness extinction. And he laid his hand on Pavlov's shoulder and kissed his cheek. Hope we didn't keep you awake last night. You could have joined in, you know. Liberate yourself. One day we're here, the next day we're not.

THEATRE, DANCE

The next morning, Pavlov was woken by the appearance of Rex the dog.

They are here, Rex said. They are both here, satisfying their instincts . . . Ah, the urge . . . I so remember these urges . . .

Pavlov took the stairs down to the street, and went looking for Son of Mechanic's car. When he located it, he paced in circles, growling and snorting and pawing the ground with his feet like a bull. Patiently, he waited for the man to return.

And there he was, walking towards his car. There was the Spartan, the son of a mechanic, the boy who had grown up surrounded by wheels and engines, caged in by tools and wrenches throughout his childhood. There he was, the graveyard fucker and dog killer, the performer of a masterpiece of eros before an audience of dead spectators who had cheered with muddy popcorn in hand, dusting the earth off their jackets, straightening their hair with holy water, applauding with bony fingers, laughing with sunken faces and absent eyes and missing teeth. Nothing could outshine a theatrical performance in the presence of that entombed crowd. Ah, the honesty of it! thought Pavlov. The courage, the brilliance. And now he, Pavlov, an admirer of ancient burial practices and Greek tragedies, was at last taking part in a play about vengeance. He would finally be onstage, yes, in a play with all the greatness and perfection of ancient theatre. The son of an undertaker finally had a role. Before the gaze of thousands of cadavers, he was about to wrestle Son of Mechanic and spill his blood in the agora. Pavlov, at last, had earned a role in the Pythian Games—he was here, standing on the half-circle stage of Dionysus, watched by legions of bare-shouldered, toga-clad mortal philosophers and lustful gods. His bleeding-nose-to-be, his future black eye, and his about-to-be-torn shirt would testify to his inclusion in the greatest tragedy ever conceived in this part of this world. Presenting *The Fertile Crescent*, ladies and gentlemen, a tragedy on the subject of pro-creation and death! All that was spoken, written and staged had foretold our eventual, inevitable extinction, and Pavlov now performed onstage before a once-upon-a-time audience, ready to receive a standing ovation from fig-shaped buttocks and olive-branch-like hands and cultured skulls thick and white as Greek yogourt.

Son of Mechanic hastened towards Pavlov and grabbed him by the throat. Pavlov held his foe's hand and wrestled him to the ground, and they fought and drew blood. Eventually Pavlov got a firm grip on Son of Mechanic and beat him mercilessly. Pavlov was strong, and had built his strength carrying cadavers on his shoulders and in his arms. He beat Son of Mechanic hard and drew blood from his eyes and nose, his split lip.

Finally his cousin's lover stood up, defeated, ran towards the trunk of his chariot, opened it and pulled out an AK-47. He pointed it at Pavlov once more.

Pavlov held his ground and laughed hysterically, a loud mocking hyena-like laugh. And then he barked. He barked at Son of Mechanic and walked away, wiping the blood off his own chin and nose. Son of Mechanic stood there panting, bewildered, aiming the rifle at Pavlov but not daring to shoot him in the back.

Back at home, Pavlov put on some music and danced. He danced for a man he'd once known and to tunes he remembered from his childhood. Moskovian, an Armenian who had lived alone across from the grocer, had played them every afternoon. The Armenian's soft music and dance tunes had enchanted Pavlov and everyone in the neighbourhood. Pavlov, as a kid, would stand under Moskovian's window to listen. Moskovian had thick glasses and hardly uttered a word. He had full, robust hair that tumbled around his face and he walked like a bear, carrying the weight of his massive body on both hips. His Arabic was broken, good enough only to get him cigarettes, his customary daily bottle of wine, and food. The grocer always corrected his grammar, laughing and teasing him. The Armenian would only nod and grab his bag of cigarettes, his wine and the food that the grocer's wife prepared for him every day.

Pavlov recalled how the Armenian had confused the feminine and masculine in his speech. He'd once referred to God in the feminine and that had become the joke of the neighbourhood. She-God, the neighbours would say, and laugh as the man crossed the street. But his music, the tunes that drifted from his window onto the street, redeemed him. He played sad, soft gypsy tunes that no one in this land had heard before and that rendered everything feminine, as if all that was masculine in Arabic—the words *gun*, *misery*, *eternity*, *home*, *ocean* and *bird*—all came out foreign, lighter, shorter, dryer from Moskovian's lips.

Once, in the evening, after all the stores were closed, Pavlov had followed his father from afar. He was curious about his father's nocturnal strolls beyond the cemetery road. He saw his father entering Moskovian's building. Pavlov went up to the roof of the grocer's store, which stood across from the Armenian's house, and watched from there. He saw his father's figure appear at the door. In the dim light, Pavlov could see his father's silhouette. He saw his father's long winter coat, his slightly curved, strong back. He watched his father stand facing the Armenian. They embraced and held elbows, then talked and paced back and forth in the room, and then they held torches of fire, and danced and swirled around each other, turning and waving the flames in their hands in vertical and horizontal motions until they both disappeared into another room and the fire ceased. All fell into darkness, all was quiet, and Pavlov stayed on the roof until he recognized the sound of his father's footsteps on the street. He rushed down the stairs and followed his father back along the cemetery road, tucking in and hiding behind rocks, trees and walls.

His father opened the graveyard gate, entered the cemetery, and stood under the direct rays of a clear moon and smoked. Then he waved at his son, and Pavlov, embarrassed and bashful, stepped out from behind the wall towards him.

What you witnessed is an act of love, said the father to his son. We worship fire because it is the closest sensation to what a man feels when love exists. Fire is a passage and a dance, but its destruction brings renewal. One day you will have to ignite my remains, but who is going to ignite yours, my son?

A few days after that, the Armenian died. That afternoon, the music stopped and the Armenian didn't come down to fetch his cigarettes, matches, food and wine.

The grocer knocked at Pavlov's father's door and asked if the Armenian had a family.

No, Pavlov's father said. He was all alone. His family perished during the Armenian genocide. He was the only survivor.

Then Pavlov's father lowered his head and said: I'll take care of it. He asked me to bury him up in the mountains. There is no need for anyone to come.

That night, Pavlov accompanied his father to the Armenian's house. He saw his father sobbing, saw him carry the corpse and lay it on a table in the middle of the main room. His father lit a fire and danced as Pavlov watched. It was a solo performance for the dead, a slow-moving dance in the Armenian's room, in honour of Moskovian. Pavlov's father performed the dance of the loner, of a man with a lit cigarette barely held between his lips, a cigarette dangling like the stray hairs of reclusive men avoiding attachments and eschewing the fragrance of ritual celebrations and burials, intoxicated by loneliness, suffocated by the closeness of others. These types of men are the hidden dark matter that exists in abundance in this universe, these kinds of men shine only in opaque corners, their deep shyness, their aloofness exorcised only through the freedom of drunkenness, their heavy eyes impersonating contemplation, their bodies swaying back and forth and sideways like worshippers. As unsteady on the floor as sarcophagi wings fluttering, these men emerge from their tombs to dance, coming alive at night in filthy places, built as shelters, with late drinking hours, and in moist basements filled with empty bottles of wine.

And after a little while, Pavlov also danced, mimicking his father. He watched his father lift Moskovian's huge body in his arms and walk down the stairs with it. Pavlov's father carried the Armenian along the secluded burial road. He walked with the dead weight augmenting gravity and the hardship caused by gravity, and took the corpse to the mortician's room. There he beautified the body. Then he loaded it in his deathmobile, and Pavlov and his father drove away and out the cemetery road towards the cremation house, to make fire and dance once again.

THE HYENA BEGS

Rifles voiced their menacing bangs in the distance. Battles are underway, Pavlov said out loud. Cadavers would again glide along the burial road, wings folded unlike birds', feet joined together unlike soldiers' boots, faces immobile unlike actors'—powdered, preserved, packaged and delivered, to be consumed by earth, gnawed by vermin and vanish again. Not only could Pavlov estimate the frequency of upcoming burials by the intensity of the bombs, he could predict the age of the dead from the location of the fighting and the targets the bombs struck. When a bombardment was directed towards the front lines, the majority of corpses would be unmarried kids, which meant the dancing type of burial. But when the bombs were aimed at civilian neighbourhoods, the processions would be the slow and solemn kind.

One day in November, his cousin the hyena appeared in Pavlov's bedroom. Before Pavlov had the chance to ask her how she had opened the main door, she wept, and fell to her knees. Her lover, Son of Mechanic, had been shot dead on the front line. Now he lay in the middle of the demarcation road. His comrades had attempted to retrieve the body, but a sniper was preventing them. His body was in no man's land, in the middle of the street, unprotected from stray dogs and opportunistic birds.

She walked on her knees towards Pavlov's bed, begging for his help. She was incoherent and choking and coughing. She grabbed Pavlov's hand and started to kiss it, pleading for his forgiveness.

Bring me the rest, Pavlov said, and I'll help you.

His cousin understood. She nodded, still weeping, and rushed down the stairs and towards the cemetery. A few minutes later she returned with a plastic bag with Rex's head inside.

Pavlov went to the kitchen, opened the fridge and laid the head next to the body.

Then he took his deathmobile from the locked garage beneath the house and drove towards the Green Line. His cousin sat beside him, whimpering, the pitch of her voice controlled by the obstruction of an overused tissue in her hand. Her hyena laugh was no more than a faint trace. Can her laugh have just disappeared? Pavlov wondered. What a creature, capable of both murder and love. He had known her all her life. He had heard her early childhood cries turn into chuckles then laughter as time reshaped her face, her breasts and her long black hair. Ah, he thought, and death has finally reached her. Nothing will be a laughing matter from now on.

He drove down the hill of Achrafieh, towards the port and the Green Line. In silence, he steered his deathmobile to the battlefield. When they reached the shipping containers, he saw the plastic chairs, empty except for a jacket, beside a bin full of coffee cups. His cousin opened the car door and ran towards the jacket. She held it to her face and sniffed it and howled. Three militia boys who recognized her took her inside the building, and Pavlov followed. Her wails echoed like birds' screeching—sharp, sad and menacing. Fighters peeked between the stairwells and through the holes in the walls. They had beards, and looked comfortable in shirts, sandals, sweatpants; some even held their rifles against their cotton pyjamas. They gathered around, drinking sodas and spitting as they went up and down the stairs, scratching their killer instincts with the tips of their rifles. To Pavlov, they seemed blasé, perhaps mildly entertained by the spectacle of a weeping woman releasing her long, breathless wails that sounded like whips or like hymns on Good Friday.

One of the militiamen, whose name was Charbel, took Pavlov up the stairs to a higher floor. Through an opening between the sandbags, he pointed out the body of Son of Mechanic. The body lay on its side in the middle of the highway, parallel to the earth and the sky, his rifle still slung across his chest. He wore dirty white sneakers and his feet were apart, legs twisted and bent, in the tradition of photos of casualties of war. The direct sunlight made Son of Mechanic appear suspended in a haze of heat that skimmed the asphalt and advanced like the waves of a nuclear blast. The body gave architectural scale to the devastation of the surrounding buildings with their bombed metal doors and pierced walls like faces punctured by a dermatologist's malpractice. A broken lamppost hunched down and sideways, leaning like a sprig of parsley or mint.

Son of Mechanic was slowly decaying, decomposing under the blazing star. His skin must be hardening in the absence of life, Pavlov thought, and sizzling under the eternal burning of the sun. The body was at a stage where it should be removed, covered and well treated. He was looking at the distant cadaver from behind the protection of bags of sand, and dust was floating everywhere. Dust, he murmured to himself, bags of dust to protect us from turning into dust. And he laughed to himself.

Charbel told Pavlov that yesterday a photographer from Spain who'd been visiting them often to take photos had brought along booze and food. They all drank, but Son of Mechanic kept on drinking after everyone else retreated. Son of Mechanic had offered to keep watch. He drank all night, then took a Kalashnikov, left the container area and ran towards the enemy line, crossing the road towards the other side, shooting and cursing. A sniper shot him right away.

We didn't even have the chance to stop him, Charbel said. We battled all morning to take back the Martyr's body, but their snipers have made it impossible. Still, we asked the headquarters for more men and we managed to make a surprise attack from the shore side. We attacked a battalion of mercenaries. Yes, Gadhafi has sent his mercenaries here. Everyone deals with this place as if it's theirs. Everyone is everything but Lebanese. Anyhow, we surprised the platoon of mercenaries.

They never thought we'd cross to the other side. But we did. We know the terrain. We grew up here. They were all huddling around a little gas stove making tea. They didn't know what hit them. Boiled water and blood was splashing against the walls. We brought a body of theirs back with us.

But we couldn't get to the Martyr. Their sniper is still covering the road. We have to get the Martyr's body before the rats and stray dogs feed on him. I picked up a loudspeaker and told the enemy that we have a body of one of their fighters and we are trying to work out an exchange, but they did not reply to us. So I hooked the fighter's body to the jeep and I dragged it around for them to see. I drove under their fire, and the sniper shot at me . . . but I drove like a madman, fast. They finally got the message and responded. We've been communicating through loudspeakers. They want us to pick up our dead friend and return their man's body, but we don't trust them. I think the moment we reach for the body, the sniper will get us. We're not sure if they give a damn about their mercenary's body.

Pavlov asked the fighter to walk back with him towards the containers. His cousin had been laid on a mattress on the ground, weeping, and when she saw Pavlov she reached for his feet and whispered, Bring him back, I want to bury him myself.

Pavlov asked the fighter if there was any way to reach Son of Mechanic by car. Yes, Charbel told him, you can access that main road by way of a small alley. Pavlov nodded. He asked the fighter to fetch a white cloth or bedsheet, and take him to the body of the mercenary.

Pavlov and Charbel untied the body from behind the jeep. The back of the mercenary's skull had cracked from bumping along the ground and part of his brain was bulging out, and the torso had been badly disfigured by the friction of the roads. They wrapped him in the sheet, leaving his face and his shoes uncovered, lifted him up and positioned him on top of the deathmobile. Then they laid a rifle at his side. Pavlov made a white flag out of a stick and some white cloth and drove the car through the alley until he reached the main road. There, he stopped.

Slowly, he opened the door. With his hands behind his head, he got out and went to stand in front of his deathmobile. He waited for death, but nothing happened. Not a shot, not a word from the loudspeakers, only a breeze from the seaside, salty air wafting from the beaches. Salt to preserve the cadavers from rotting, he thought, a lost, ancient art that should be revived. Salt, he thought, and he kept his eyes on the ground and repeated, Salt, the eye of the Medusa, pillars of salt . . . And he thought he should cover Rex's remains in salt, and he thought of all the salt in the ocean and on earth . . . White, coarse, crystal-like salt for Rex. The idea pleased him and he smiled.

He stood in the middle of the road that divided Beirut in half. An empty two-way road that separated two fighting militias. A long road that sliced vertically through the city and stretched towards the seas. On both sides were blown-up stores, assaulted street lamps standing in the manner of hunchbacks in a famine. There were abandoned cars and mortar holes in the ground and traces of bullets everywhere.

Pavlov turned his head carefully and saw fortifications made of sandbags and shipping containers on both sides. The containers blocked the roads, as did the sandbags, and burned-out vehicles and weeds were sprouting everywhere through asphalt and walls. Grass grew everywhere: in the sandbags, on the roofs of the small stores, between the old beaten arches, on top of the columns lying on the ground . . . He was in no man's land and he thought about his own death, the death of his dog and the devastation of fire.

Slowly, he approached Son of Mechanic, reached down and dragging the body by the feet, walked back towards the small alley. There, Pavlov laid Son of Mechanic on the sidewalk, within reach of his comrades.

He returned to his deathmobile, got in and began to drive slowly towards the other side.

ACTING

The body of the mercenary was still tied to the roof of the deathmobile. Pavlov drove straight across the demarcation road.

He reached the other side of the city, parked his car and waited at the entrance to a street that had its end blocked by a large shipping container. Two fighters stuck their heads out of a door in the middle of the street and summoned him with a nod of their heads and a half-circular gesture with their guns. He drove along the open street and waited beside the container at the end of it.

Two militiamen appeared from an opening in the side of the container, guns pointed at him. They were shouting as they brandished their rifles in his face. Get down on the ground, they yelled, and he knelt. He noticed their beards, their jeans and loose T-shirts. From the ground he watched their sandals and their thick military boots going back and forth. He remained where he was, with his hands on his head.

One of the militiamen put a boot on Pavlov's back and frisked him, while his companion quickly looked inside the car.

Get up!

Pavlov got up.

Two more fighters rushed out and unloaded the cadaver. Then someone blindfolded Pavlov and dragged him through an opening between two shipping containers.

Pavlov sat on a chair, waiting, while the fighters discussed the fate of the mercenary's body. They were arguing.

Do you have the body's papers? one of the men finally asked Pavlov.

No, Pavlov answered.

How did you get the body?

I was called to help.

Pavlov could barely glimpse this man's uniform under his blindfold but guessed he too must be a mercenary, one of Gadhafi's brigade. They are always wandering, lost, he thought to himself, and smiled.

Let's see what the madman here has to tell us. One of the boots turned to Pavlov and walked towards him. Suddenly he was grabbed by the hair, slapped and then pushed to the ground. Someone started to stomp on him. Pavlov moaned under the blows of the heavy boots. The stomping was not frequent, nor rhythmic. It was not even hateful. Pavlov detected hesitation.

Another fighter intervened, pushed the first man away from Pavlov and ordered him to stand up. He dragged Pavlov to a room inside an empty building. It echoed and had a pungent smell of dampness. The man pushed Pavlov to the floor and pulled up a large, empty olive oil can to sit on. He placed it so he faced Pavlov, and tore off his blindfold.

So, what should we call you? he asked.

Pavlov.

The man burst out laughing. Are you Russian?

No, I am from here.

Is that your war name, Pavlov?

No.

You are Christian?

I am not a believer, Pavlov said. He could sense the man's surprise.

So you're a Communist.

No.

Then what do you believe in?

I believe in dogs.

The man's laughter echoed in the empty building. You believe in dogs?

Yes.

You worship dogs?

No.

Are you a madman?

If I was, Pavlov replied, I wouldn't be able to tell.

So what are you?

I am an undertaker, and the son of an undertaker.

You don't look like an undertaker. You look too young to be an undertaker. You look like a fighter to me. You're young and have long hair, and Pavlov is your assumed war

RAWI HAGE ~ 196

name. And judging by your broad, strong shoulders, I think you've done some military training.

No, said Pavlov. I have broad shoulders from digging graves.

Did you volunteer to pick up the body or did they pay you?

I volunteered.

So you are definitely Christian. Christians love to volunteer. The man started to laugh. But you said you're not a believer.

No.

Yet you believe in dogs.

I believe that they are superior to humans.

Why did you do it, dog man? We could have shot you as well. I watched you picking up the body. Is he a relative of yours?

Who? asked Pavlov.

The mad fighter who ran towards us. Cursing us and our mothers. My men were about to shoot you. I stopped them. You know why?

No.

Because I was curious about what was going on in your head. I wanted to know why a man would do such a thing for another man, a dead man.

I did it because I wanted them to stop dragging the body. Hector didn't deserve his body to be dragged around.

So the dead man is Hector.

No.

Who is Hector?

The Greek warrior.

You have Greeks fighting with you?

No. I was referring to Homer.

What Homer?

The writer.

You're a nutcase, man! Was your dead friend on drugs? He rushed towards us in the middle of the night.

I don't know.

You must know something. Why are you risking your life for this man?

My father was an undertaker, Pavlov said, and now I am an undertaker.

I don't believe you, the fighter said. I think you did it because you know the dead man. You want to bury him. Who is the woman wailing on the other side? Are you doing it for the woman?

I am doing it because my father would have done it.

Your father, meaning your Christian father? Like the father of Jesus?

No.

You can tell me. My mother is Christian, I know about your so-called Father. I am sure that you know how to use a gun, right? Have you fired a gun, Pavlov?

Yes, my uncle showed me how.

The man started to laugh loudly. You know how to use a gun. You're not an undertaker. You're a fighter. You just said so.

My father was an undertaker and so am I.

I think you're a combatant. The man slapped Pavlov, hard. You know, you're not dead yet because I like you, I like your courage and madness. But you have to tell me the truth or I am going to shoot you and throw your body to the dogs that you love so much.

As Pavlov was about to reply, a second fighter burst into the room.

Big Moustafa is here, he informed his comrade. Do you want us to hand him the Libyan's body?

My father knows Big Moustafa, Pavlov said quickly. Big Moustafa the undertaker has his funeral home in Ain al-Mreisseh, he added. Big Moustafa will testify that I am the son of an undertaker. He knew my father before the war. My father talked about him. Big Moustafa visited our home before the war.

Pavlov's interrogator said, Bring Big Moustafa in here.

Big Moustafa, the undertaker, lived up to his name. He had a long white beard and a humongous round belly, and wore suspenders over his T-shirt. His belt barely stopped his belly from falling to his knees.

This young man claims that you knew his father.

Who's your father? Big Moustafa asked.

Who's your father? the fighter repeated.

Awad the undertaker, Pavlov said.

Awad from Mar Mitr over in Achrafieh! Moustafa laughed. Yes, I know this man's father. How is he, son?

Dead, Pavlov said.

May he rest in warmth and peace. I'll tell you a story about him. Years ago, I spent the funniest day with your father. And then he invited me to dinner at your house. You were a kid back then. But before I go on . . . what are you doing over here, anyway?

I picked up a body, Pavlov said.

Oh, good man, you took over the business. My sons won't touch the profession. They all ran away. You're doing a great honour to your father. He was a decent chap.

Big Moustafa turned to address the militiamen: I know this man and his family, he declared. I, Big Moustafa, I am talking to all of you. I, Big Moustafa, have buried many of your friends and family. I am Big Moustafa the undertaker who has washed your beloveds' bodies and wrapped them in soft cloth and helped you bury them. Now I am asking you to give this young man some water. This man is our guest. Where are your manners? Your dead will shame you if you disrespect my wishes and I'll never touch any of your bodies if you get killed. Hear me, O people. When you die, I will bury you in dirt and never wash you clean to meet your maker.

Now you all listen to my story, said Big Moustafa. A long time ago, this man's father and I were both asked to arrange the funeral of a Muslim man who had converted to Christianity. His wife was Christian. When he died, his wife and her family wanted to give him a Christian burial, but his brothers and parents wanted a Muslim ceremony. The parents told me to go to the village with them and bring the body back home. We drove up somewhere in the mountains towards the Christian villages of Kfar Matta. This was before the war . . . So here we were, this young undertaker's father and myself, representing two different religions and waiting for the family to settle their feud, wondering which of us would leave with the body. The wife refused to give the body to the parents. She said that her husband had converted and his final wish was to be buried as a Christian. But the young man's father begged the wife to give him the body and move on. She didn't have any kids, she was still young and beautiful—she could always remarry and get on with her life.

The young widow suggested a compromise: that her husband be buried in a Christian cemetery but his body be washed according to Muslim rites. He could be wrapped in a white cloth according to Muslim tradition and be buried with his head facing Mecca. The stone would have only his name and dates, and no cross or Fateha. The father requested that a sheik be brought to perform the prayers, and the woman said she wouldn't mind having a sheik as long as a priest was also present at the burial.

The burial lasted hours. The priest offered the sheik the first prayer, but the sheik declined and insisted that the priest start the prayers since this was his home village, upon which the priest insisted that although the village might be Christian, it still upheld the old traditions of Arab hospitality. The sheik replied that he was eager to hear the priest's beautiful voice and the prayers of Issa, Jesus, whom he acknowledged as one of the prophets of Islam. This debate by the gravesite went on for over an hour, with discussion and false courtesies, each clergyman trying to outmanoeuvre the other so that he could recite his religion's prayer last and thereby seal the fate of the dead in either heaven. In the end, the priest was compelled to go first and give the sheik the last prayer, and not utter a word more. But when the sheik was done, the priest splashed some holy water on the grave. The sheik followed with another prayer. For the next three hours, the priest and the sheik stood above the dead man trading rituals and prayers until at last your father went up to them both and said, I will count to three and you will both stop at the same time, and whoever doesn't I am going to shove down the hole and bury with the dead.

Big Moustafa laughed, his belly bouncing. He turned to the fighter and said, Let him go, for God's sake. Let him go. These are good people. I know his family. The man's only earning a living and he brought you one of yours at the risk of his own life. It was a fair exchange.

Before Pavlov drove his car back across the demarcation line, Big Moustafa asked him to come to his hearse to sign some witness papers.

They sat in the car and Big Moustafa shared a broad smile with Pavlov. Son, you believe in the value of fire and light over the filth of the earth?

Pavlov nodded.

Son, you took over from your father. Let me kiss your head. How is your father's furnace that I heard so much about? If you need any spare parts, here's my number. Call me. I know a man who imports parts from Germany—I could send them to you across the line. There are still a few people who seek to return to the abode of fire and to leave this earthly pigsty. Let me kiss your head again, son. Nothing pleases me more than seeing a son of the fire and light.

Pavlov walked back to his own hearse and drove away from the narrow street. He crossed the divide, the long road that separated the two sides of the city. He drove his deathmobile over broken glass, falling stones from the shelled buildings and the abundant weeds that peeked from underneath the old asphalt, and arrived back in the same narrow street on the Christian side.

Two militiamen greeted him. He parked, got out and walked towards the plastic chairs, where his cousin was still wailing beside Son of Mechanic's body. Pavlov tried to pull her away, but she clung to the corpse, held it in her arms and screamed. Finally a militiaman dragged her away forcibly. She shook her head in protest, and her hair flew and lashed the faces of Pavlov and the soldier. She leaned forwards towards her lover and pulled hard, dragging the fighter along with her.

Pavlov stepped between her and the body, and placed a tender hand on her face. He whispered in her ear, It's time for the dead to dance.

REX REDUX

The following night, Pavlov removed his dog from the fridge. He carried the two bags outside, laid them in the back of his deathmobile and drove into the high mountains of his youth. The deathmobile climbed steadily through the hills and along the small roads, passing villages and stone churches.

He arrived at the cremation house at a late hour, after midnight. He reached for the key under the vase and opened the door. He took Rex the dog out of the hearse, and gently laid him on the wooden stretcher his father had built with his own hands.

Then he sat on the sofa and conversed with his dog. They both drank what was left from the bottle in his father's cupboard and Rex tried to howl with difficulty.

Finally, Pavlov lit the furnace, and bade farewell to his companion. He repositioned the head and the body of the dog to make them one and whole again, and eased him into the furnace. He slowly closed the door and went out for some fresh air.

Three hours, he thought, and shed a few tears.

He lit a cigarette and watched the stars circling in abundance over dark stretches on the surface film of sky, suspended and flattened with the simplicity of a medieval map—its unremarkable edge, and its abyss for man to fall into, screaming in horror.

Sparks from the flames, little dots all around him, confirmed for him his father's belief in the beauty of fire and the supremacy of light. But suddenly the sky turned dark. A sea of mist rose from the valley below and veiled all that glittered and shone. Alongside the mist, a silence surfaced, and the man who loved dogs could hear his own pulse, a steady rhythm that rose with the wet invasion and fell with the cold air. Only Pavlov's cigarette shone now, like a solitary star. He waited, solemn and immobile. All this shall pass, he thought, and he looked for his matches to ignite another star.

Two hours passed and Pavlov stood his ground in the grey sheet of mist. The damp filled his hair, his clothes and mouth. He was covered in dew. Water, Pavlov thought, also passes away. Towards early morning a faint light broke at the horizon behind the hills and liquidated the opaque mist. Birds called, plants unveiled their colours to the world, and magnificent scenery appeared.

Pavlov compared this vast view of the mountains with the one from his balcony in Beirut. He thought: My window view is morbid and limited. Maybe it was time to contemplate an escape from inherited sadnesses. Last night he had witnessed dying stars, the last light they exhaled before, per-haps, reaching a planet ruled by monkeys who had perfected the arts of papermaking, fire and smoking cigarettes. He thought of water again, and then of dust, and then remem-bered the furnace and Rex turning to ash. He looked at his watch. One more cigarette.

He was tired and wanted to sleep, but had to be back for Son of Mechanic's funeral. Other than that and his promises to the Society, he realized, he was free of obligations. All that had bound him was affection for a lost madwoman and the company of a dog—and both were gone.

He went back into the house, drank water and opened the furnace to let it cool. Rex had disappeared. All that was left of him was dust and small traces of a dog's bones. He gathered the ashes and put them in a plastic bag. Then he sat outside again with a glass of whisky and a can of beans.

After a while, he walked along his father's path through the bushes and over large rocks. He balanced at the edge of the cliff. He sniffed, searching for the wind's direction. He poured the remains of Rex down the slope and into the steep, deep valley. He thought how the dog would enjoy this flight; even Rex's former companion, Tariq the flying war-rior, would approve.

A little later, Pavlov locked the door behind him, slipped the house key under the vase and walked away from the House of Ashes.

WINTER

DANCING

In the early morning in Beirut, Pavlov sat on his balcony and smoked. Then he went down to the cemetery and stood by his parents' graves. Soon, he said to his father, I'll exhume your body and light you a magnificent fire. Soon, he said, when the eyes of my uncles are not watching me, I will liberate you from the heaviness of mud and burn you to ashes. He lit another cigarette and walked back to his balcony and stayed there until he heard the first tuning note, the note that presaged a chorus and began the burial dance. Tears for Son of Mechanic starting to flow.

Oh, the sound! A trumpet started it, followed by loud drums and cymbals. Pavlov went into the bathroom to wash his face and comb his hair. He grabbed his white shirt and black tie and hurried down onto the street. His cousin had hired a new band to play at her funeral-wedding to Son of Mechanic. She was all in white, with a white lace handkerchief and flowers in her hair. Pavlov joined his two uncles and the group of fighters, his feet tapping to the new repertoire of death tunes. As the band crescendoed and the drums boomed, Pavlov danced, carrying the coffin on his shoulder, grabbing a handle with one hand and waving his other hand in the air, stomping and smiling, laughing and jumping in the sunlight. In the middle of it all, he let out a loud howl and danced.

That night and the next, he listened to his cousin's lamenting laughter as she roamed the cemetery. The sound bounced between her house and the cemetery gate and her lover's headstone. On the second night, Pavlov went out and stood on his balcony, watching her white robe as it flowed inside the cemetery in the manner of ghosts and desert jinn.

Near midnight, two motorcycles appeared below his balcony. Pavlov grabbed his coat and car keys and went down to meet them. He saluted Hanneh and Manneh, who informed him that Jean Yacoub, the man who had lost his son at the hands of a warlord named Assaf, had died. Pavlov nodded, and made his way over to the garage that housed the deathmobile.

What had happened to Jean Yacoub was this: He had waited in his car at the end of the street where he knew Assaf's motorcade would appear. The moment he saw the metal door of the gate opening, he got out of his car and walked towards it. He waited on the sidewalk for the first car to exit the gate, then pulled out his gun and aimed it at the tinted rear window. But Assaf the warlord had a habit of sitting next to the driver in the front, and he escaped the attempt to kill him. Jean Yacoub was gunned down on the sidewalk in front of the building where his son had been shot. The bodyguard emptied three rounds into him. The blood that escaped his body gathered on the cement and formed a small pool, then gained momentum and ran down the edge to where the sidewalk and the asphalt met. It formed a thick, long line along the road, and for days afterwards people crossed back and forth above the sidewalk without noticing the dark colour of defeat.

Hanneh and Manneh had the papers for the morgue. They retrieved Jean's body and helped Pavlov lay the corpse in the deathmobile. All three men, and the cadaver, drove to the cremation house.

Jean Yacoub was burned in the house, and his ashes were gathered and carried to the cliff where one wind or another was bound to pass. Hanneh and Manneh sprinkled his ashes where Pavlov's father had once sprinkled those of Jean's son. Then Pavlov and his friends ate and drank in his memory before turning around and driving back to the city.

The next morning Pavlov noticed a fly trapped inside his window. It buzzed and bumped against the glass, frantic, its wings refracting rays from the winter sun that shone on Beirut and, he assumed, on other parts of the world. Pavlov leaned against the wall of his living room and watched, hesitant, hoping that the fly would discover the crack in the glass and be saved from its entrapment. He approached it with a newspaper in hand, and directed it towards the crack in the glass, but the fly became frantic again and beat its wings loudly against the window until finally it reached the opening and escaped in the direction of the distant trees. Fear comes before emancipation, and frenzy before flight, Pavlov declared to the memory of Rex.

The ceiling fan started to spin again, announcing the return of the electric current. Pavlov opened his closet and reached for his wrinkled shirt, set out the ironing board, removed the iron and began to shape the white fabric in straight lines. The fan stopped and the electricity cut out just as he was about to hang his shirt back in the closet. He went to the bathroom and checked the water pressure. Feeble. He counted his plastic razors, and positioned his shaving brush within reach of the mirror, the soap by its side. He grabbed his shoes and polished them.

All this done, he stepped out onto his balcony and waited for the tolling of the bells. The weak sun hit his face and he wondered if the fly was aware of the relationship between interior and exterior, if it contemplated the question of false transparencies or ever asked why the visible universe could not be attained because of the treachery of glass, if it was grateful to Pavlov for his grand act of altruism. Fear and mis-understanding between man and other creatures is common, he thought. The fly, he remarked to the sun, in its great terror, must have thought that I wanted to capture and devour it, and surely believed it had won its emancipation by its own heroism and ingenuity. I, the fly proclaimed, escaped this fantastical entrapment through my skill in flying and the persistence of my will! Idiotic fly, Pavlov mumbled to the sun, suddenly vexed and saddened by the ingratitude of all creatures and by the vastness and loneliness of the cosmos.

His thoughts turned to his sister Nathalie, up in the mountains. Perhaps he should visit her and her husband and their daughter, five years old by now. He wondered if his sister read to her daughter or if, instead, she contributed to her daughter's entrapment in a world composed of the butcher's ignorance and her own joyless practicality. Maybe, he thought, he could help liberate his niece—a small directional movement, and then she might be capable of grand, liberating flight?

FAMILY OUTING

P avlov took his deathmobile, which had always been a source of misery and shame to his sister, and went to visit her. On the way, he stopped and bought a doll, sweets, bread, picture books, a basket of fruit, two bottles of Johnnie Walker (the red kind), a dress for his sister and a silk scarf. He drove along the coast and north, and before he arrived at the city port of Jounieh he took a turn uphill towards the mountainous region.

When Pavlov arrived at the village, he parked in the centre and walked towards Nathalie's house with his bags of gifts. At the gate, a dog growled. Joseph glanced up but didn't recognize Pavlov—or maybe he had forgotten about his brother-in-law's existence. In any case, he didn't call off the dog and continued working on his car, its parts scattered on the ground. The dog began barking threats, so Pavlov ordered him to fetch his sister, and the dog obeyed. In no time, Nathalie came out and ran towards him, berating her husband for not opening the gate where Pavlov stood, bags in hand.

The husband barely greeted Pavlov and returned to working on his car, but his niece, Rima, watched shyly from the porch as Pavlov advanced with a large smile. His sister accepted his gifts and kissed him. She shouted out to her husband: You didn't even recognize my brother! Lucky that Barbus is here to announce his coming, or you would have left him to stand unwelcome at the gate.

Pavlov noticed that Joseph had gained weight. He took in the butcher's strong hands, his loose pants with a waist that reached above his belly button and cuffs that hovered above the ankles, and his style of shoes that hadn't changed since Pavlov had last seen him at work, standing with a piece of chopped meat or the head of a goat in his hand.

Pavlov gently approached his niece and brought out the books and the doll, and offered them to her. She smiled. He took her in his arms and kissed her.

Joseph watched all this, reserved but not hostile. Like many villagers, he met the arrival of city people with uncertainty or indifference, and eventually a hint of amusement. But Pavlov's sister was unusually affectionate. She had a new, motherly look to her. Her hips had widened, and her long skirt and red cheeks helped her blend in with her agrarian surroundings. Even her voice was louder now. She was very excited to see Pavlov, and she didn't hold back her enthusiasm. She brought him coffee and seemed appreciative of his gifts, touched that Pavlov, her self-absorbed little brother, the bookworm who had talked only about antiquity, had grown up to become a thoughtful uncle.

You bought all these things? she asked in an uncertain tone that fell between a question, affection and approval. I guess the dead Greeks in those books didn't totally dim your mind! Look at you. For once you remember us.

Over dinner, Pavlov told his sister that on his way to the village he had noticed a large convoy of military trucks going uphill. It seems they are preparing for a battle, he said.

Joseph replied that he had already spoken to the commander of the region, and the commander, a second cousin, had assured him that the military presence nearby was a precautionary measure, and purely for training purposes. No battle would be fought there.

Then why are they bringing trucks full of sand and sandbags? asked Pavlov. They are clearly planning fortifications.

A silence ensued, and everyone except little Rima fixed their eyes on the table.

At last his sister, in a low voice, continued. In any case, we won't be here for long. We've decided to leave the country. I've been meaning to let you know but never got around to it, with all the work and the kid . . . We have our visas and are just waiting for Joseph to fix the car and sell it, and then we will be gone. It's for our girl, for our Rima.

Pavlov smiled a brief ambiguous smile and gave a long nod as he reached for a piece of bread. He broke it but didn't eat it.

Joseph's brother and his family are already in Sweden, Nathalie said. There is a large Syriac community in Stockholm now. His brother has a good business and he asked us to come. He sponsored us. It's better for the future.

And the house? Pavlov asked.

Oh, we will be back one day, when the war is over.

His little niece approached Pavlov with her book, and he lifted her onto his knee. He opened it and she pointed to a page, and he read to her.

<hr />

The next morning a large explosion was heard, followed by gunshots, the movement of military trucks, and shouting. Suddenly bombs started to rain down.

Pavlov's sister rushed to her daughter's room, wailing. Joseph ran out of the house, bewildered, looking for an explanation. He crossed the road in his thick cotton pyjamas, running barefoot towards the gate, and waved to a car with four militiamen inside, their rifles sticking out of the windows.

Pavlov stood just outside the front door, trying to determine where the shots had come from. His sister stood behind him in an opaque wool nightgown, her child weeping in her arms.

Joseph charged back to the house. He seemed angry—not fearful but angry—and paced back and forth between inside and outside. Finally he said, There is an attack on the village.

Pavlov's sister clutched Rima in panic, and her daughter quickly became drenched in tears. Joseph took Rima and ran outside once more. Nathalie followed, taking the old stone stairs that led through the garden and down into a cave beneath the house. Pavlov stayed above for a while, listening to the proximity of the shots, watching as the valleys produced little mushrooms of smoke that seemed to burst from the earth itself. Then a bomb landed very close by and he heard his sister screaming to him, begging him to join them in the basement. He grabbed a quilt and bottles of water, opened the fridge and gathered some food, scooped up his niece's doll and books, and went underground with the rest of the family.

All day and night, into the next morning, mortars and guns exchanged fire. Pavlov and the family were stranded, ignorant of what was taking place in the village above. When Joseph attempted to leave the basement, Pavlov's sister stood at the door begging him to stay and wait for a ceasefire. After a while Rima began calling for their dog, Barbus, who was missing. The butcher pushed past Nathalie and went outside, and came back with more food and two weapons, a hunting rifle and a handgun. He reported that the dog was nowhere to be seen. He stood just outside the door to the cave, and Pavlov joined him. They looked out at the valley, searching for clues about what was happening. Bullets and small artillery landed close by, but Pavlov and Joseph remained where they were, feeling protected behind a pillar and beside a large oak tree that partially covered the entrance. The back-and-forth move-ment of trucks and tanks could be heard, climbing the road.

The militia is on the move, Joseph said. Uphill. Towards the monastery.

They felt the vibrations of tanks and watched as these vehicles passed beside the house, raising dust and bending the branches that overhanged the narrow village roads. Joseph propped his hunting rifle against the wall of the cave and ran to meet the tanks. Pavlov followed, and they both ducked into the yard and stopped by the gate, waving and shouting at the jeep behind the tank. What's going on? they shouted, but the soldiers were distracted and didn't reply. At last one of them answered, but Pavlov and his brother-in-law couldn't hear because the tank was so loud as it passed along the small curved road. They both stood stupefied, staring at the tracks the big machine had imprinted in the asphalt.

We should leave, Pavlov said, but as the words left his lips more bombs started to fall, and he and Joseph fled back towards the cave, retreating like miserable hunched foxes at the coming of a storm.

For three more days, they were trapped in the basement. His sister prayed and wept, and Rima clung to her mother, falling asleep occasionally. At other times she would wake and sense the tension and fear in her mother's body, and she would cry and call the dog's name again and again. The few trips Pavlov managed to make up to the house to fetch food almost got him killed. The fighting was closer now, and he had to crawl on his hands and knees into the kitchen.

In his preoccupation with collecting food, Pavlov had forgotten to grab the radio, so at last, after nightfall, he crawled back up the stairs and re-entered the house. It was pitch-black, but to strike a match or press an electric switch would bring a hail of bullets and bombs. He crawled along the floor, feeling for walls and the edges of furniture, his hand reaching beneath tables and counters. Finally he stumbled upon wires and, following them, he located the fridge, stove and even a blow-dryer. Broken glass lay everywhere. A fragment pierced his palm as he reached for the radio, but he grabbed it, bleeding over its dial. He carried it down to the basement. There he turned it on, and an old song played, the sound resonating inside the concave walls.

Finally the news came on. Two Christian factions had started fighting each other up in the hills, and their battleground was the village. A moment of pride came to Joseph upon hearing the name of his little, barely known village, Kfaroumeh, but this was cut short by fear.

Now we know, he said. Two Christian factions. He lit a cigarette. What for? Fighting among ourselves. It's time to leave. Maybe we could walk down the valley. Leave the house and car and just walk down.

Pavlov objected, as did his sister, whose voice came out from an invisible, dark corner. The only sound was her faint protesting voice, and her child's breathing.

Pavlov turned the radio off. To save batteries, he said.

Soon, the battle escalated. Bombs fell with an unprecedented frequency, and all noise, songs, voices, murmurs and complaints were subdued, crushed by the sound. The family moved deeper within their cave, to the farthest corner, and crouched in silence, oblivious to the dampness of the walls. In their helplessness, they assumed an instinctive frozen posture, the still form of rabbits in the presence of a predator. Other than the bombs, there was utter silence.

At dawn on the third day, Pavlov felt briefly reassured by the arrival of a crack of light—but this moment was interrupted by the sudden entrance of a fighter into the cave.

The man rushed in and fell to the floor, his back against the damp, cold wall. He was panting and moaning in pain. The morning sun shed a faint light on the side of his face, and the first thing that struck Pavlov was the sharpness of his long nose that was channelling air in urgent and fast intervals. Then he heard the man's cries. Pavlov stood and approached him. The fighter was bleeding from the neck. Pavlov retreated, grabbed the little water that was left in the family's bottle and offered it to him. The man tried, but couldn't swallow. He rejected the liquid that entered his mouth and coughed. Pavlov poured water into his hand and washed the man's face. The water revealed the fighter's youth, his boyish looks, his regret and fear. His eyes showed that he had been crying for a long time—and being touched with such care made him cry more. He was bleeding from his arm as well as his throat. He pulled a photo from his pocket and put it against his chest. He tried to talk but had no voice, and only a few obscure, weak whistles emerged, accompanied by drooling blood and tears. Then he stopped moving, took a final short breath and ceased.

Pavlov laid him flat on the ground. Now the fighter looked more dignified. The dead, when laid horizontally beneath whatever happens to be above, can face anything, he thought. A panorama of high-rises, chandeliers, high or low ceilings, solemn faces—rain and sometimes clouds, or blue skies if they were fortunate enough.

Joseph grew angry again. What for? he said. What are they killing each other for? We can't leave the body here.

Pavlov's sister wept when she heard the word *body*—and Rima, too, started to wail.

We can't leave him here, Joseph repeated.

Hours later, when the fighting seemed to have paused, Pavlov began to drag the corpse out of the cave. Joseph grabbed the dead fighter's hand, and together they carried him outside the cave.

The wild dogs will come at night, Joseph said. My daughter will get sick. She is already half-dead and traumatized and she hasn't seen the light in days. We could bury him, but it will take time to dig the grave and we will be exposed to snipers and mad fire. They will take us for soldiers and shoot us, and the shovels in our hands will look like weapons . . . they will shoot us . . . What for? Joseph said once again. What for?

And without another word, Joseph rushed to his car and returned with a tank of gas. Pavlov helped him carry the body to the field and they laid it out, facing the sky. Joseph poured gas on it.

Go back, Pavlov said, before someone notices the flames and shoots us. Joseph nodded and headed to the cave.

Pavlov took his time. He gathered hay, twigs and broken branches and piled them over the fighter's body. He lit the branches and stood watching the birth of fire, and then he circled the pyre, mourning and dancing for the unknown.

That night, when the fighting had quieted and the bombs had paused, Pavlov went to look for his bag in the darkness of the kitchen above. He found it, picked up his car keys, left the house, walked through the gate and downhill on the village road. He held his keys firmly in his hands, not in his pocket, for fear that the jingling sound might awaken the killers. He passed the few stores of the village, his brother-in-law's butcher shop, the grocery and a café. All were empty, bombarded or looted, and broken glass was everywhere, on the sidewalks and in the middle of the road. A long spire-shaped rowan tree blocked the moonlight and its reflection drew an oval, dark figure, boat-like, across the scattered shards on the ground. He continued down the slope towards his hearse. In the dark, he didn't notice its shattered windshield until he sat on the broken glass on the seat. A piece pierced his thigh, but he kept quiet, calmly inserted the key, started the engine and drove up the road towards his sister's house.

When he arrived, he took the flashlight from the car and went down to the basement. Joseph was snoring, and Pavlov's niece's body had slipped out from under the quilt. Rima looked cold, hungry and thirsty against the blackness of the wall. His sister lay beside her, and Pavlov imagined the expression of devastation on her face. He turned the flashlight on and woke them.

Our father's car is here, he told his sister, we must leave now.

The butcher objected, but Pavlov's sister immediately started to pack, mumbling, Trust in the will of God, trust the mercy of the saints . . . With no food or water, we are buried here anyway, she said. We might as well take our chances outside.

Nathalie covered her daughter with the quilt, and went quickly up the stairs. Meanwhile, Joseph entered the darkness of his house, grabbed the family's passports and stuffed a bag with clothes. They all hurried into the hearse. Pavlov's niece was awake now and asking after the dog. No one answered her. Nathalie sat with her daughter in the back and they drove down the hill.

It was a cold mountain morning, and the broken windshield let the air into the quiet interior, ventilating the vehicle, which was full of the odours of these unwashed humans. Nathalie huddled with her daughter, and Joseph sat anxiously in the front passenger seat, looking around and through the open angles of glass in the window. Upon passing the stores in the village, he murmured, The business! Everything is gone, all is destroyed . . . What for?

Pavlov drove the deathmobile down the hill until he met a checkpoint marked by flickering torches. He stopped, and two fighters with AK-47s approached and skimmed their flashlights over the faces in the car before tracing the forms of their bodies and the inside of the hearse. One fighter recognized Joseph and greeted him. The fighter was a kid, barely sixteen, and he and Joseph were distantly related. The butcher asked him which road was the safest, and he advised the family to take the northern road and go east until the next large town, and from there head south towards the city.

Do you have any food? the fighter asked. Pavlov's sister, her voice rising from the back seat, told him to go to their house and take anything he could find.

The butcher guided Pavlov along the roads until dawn, when the sun revealed all and little Rima began screaming the name of her dog, pointing at a stray creature at the side of the road. Pavlov stopped. The dog was trotting aimlessly. It looked thin, dirty, hungry and fearful, its skin peeling. Its eyes were sunken in its head and its nose pointed at the earth, as if defeated and ashamed. Barbus, the girl called, Barbus! And the canine turned, and wagged its tail with happiness. It rushed back to the car and settled in the back of the death-mobile and rested, filthy and smelly, in the little girl's arms.

—•—

The hearse arrived safely back in the city and the family stayed for a couple of weeks in the home that looked out over the cemetery road. One day the butcher and his wife walked to the grocer's to buy food. Rima stayed at the house with her uncle and sat with her dog on the sofa. She asked if Pavlov was coming to Sweden with them.

Pavlov told her that he and Barbus would stay behind, because the dog would not be able to take the boat to Cyprus with them when they left. Pavlov promised that he would protect Barbus and feed him well.

The note of a trumpet sounded, and Pavlov went to the window. The girl stood beside him. She said, The dead are coming.

The dead are coming, Pavlov repeated.

But where do they go?

To Hades, Pavlov said.

Who is there in Hades?

Pluto, Pavlov said.

Is he nice?

He likes to live in the underworld, Pavlov said.

And where is God? Rima asked.

There is no God, there are only humans who imagine the possibility of gods.

When the music started, Pavlov went to the middle of the room and moved his feet. The dog joined him. He extended his arms to his little niece, and all three of them danced to the tune of the dead.

AU REVOIR?

Throughout December, rain and bombs continued to fall on Beirut and its inhabitants. Mortals sought the shelter of the underworld: people slept in their underground garages, in utility rooms, next to meters and electrical boxes, in commercial storage spaces, in factories and church crypts, and in hell. Bombs carpeted the roofs, spliced little streets, landed on coiffed heads and leather-clad feet, spilled human entrails and turned their bodies into butcher's meat—chuck steak, rib, lower sirloin, flank, shoulder. Bombs sharpened the edges of windows and pierced the smooth surfaces of walls, scattered an apocalypse of stones and furniture. Glass covered the street and gleamed in the sun—glitter with the motion of oceans. The wrath of the Gods fell even on the dead. The lawns of the cemetery across from Pavlov's window were prodded by bombs and thunderous explosions, and mortars landed on graves and ploughed the ground. Skeletons, like playful dolphins, flew out of the earth and pirouetted through the air to land again in the mud. A buried grocer's bones were resurrected and piled in the manner of a vegetable display. A real estate agent's body flew in the air and landed in the next lot of land. A pharmacist with a headache found oblivion in an open field, a long-dead fighter was wounded once again, and still the bombs persisted, falling in a pitiless avalanche, excavating the ancient Roman city under the surface. The names of the deceased were misspelled on bombed headstones, statues of virgins were riddled with holes and lost their reputations for immaculate conception. The dead screamed in terror, from the end of the street came a loud hyena laugh, and in Pavlov's rooms the memory of Rex the dog's howl echoed.

With the end of the bombing came the second burial of those long dead and forgotten, those whose rest in peace, slumber and decomposition had been rudely interrupted by the impudence of the living. Pavlov left his sister's family at home, and walked with his uncles through the burial grounds, gathering bones and human remains and returning them to the earth. Broken headstones were restored to the tops of their proper plots. The shredding of wreaths had scattered flowers and petals on the ground, filling the cemetery with Indian summer colours. His cousin, the hyena, arrived with her brother and sniffed the earth. She looked at Pavlov with grateful eyes, and he observed that she seemed broken and somewhat older now. The shape of her face no longer had the geometric perfection of eternity. Worry and sadness had thinned it into the shape of a triangle. The Pythagorean cult and its trinities can be seen everywhere in this land, Pavlov observed—in

triangular noses, triangular chins, triangular mountains . . .
The hyena's little brother walked the rows with the familiar-
ity of a child in a playground, and both siblings softly hummed
old, folkloric songs to appease the cadavers.

When his work was done, Pavlov returned home. He
washed his hands, his face and neck, and the sink filled with
earth and the pale colour of bones and the brown of his own
skin. Now, he said to himself, it is time for my sister and her
family to leave. They ought to leave now.

The next day, Pavlov drove his sister's family to the port to
catch the boat that would take them to the island of Cyprus.
From there, they would fly to Sweden and join Joseph's family.
Nathalie cried as they drove. I always hated this car, she said
to Pavlov. Sell everything and come with us.

His niece begged him to bring Barbus with him when
he came north. The butcher, smelling of sweat and with tears
in his eyes, hugged and kissed Pavlov, emitting heat from his
large body.

Pavlov kissed them all and said goodbye. As he drove back
home alone, he thought: Now I must attend to the life of a
new dog.

FADDOUL

Later that night, a faint knock struck Pavlov's door. Then
a stone bounced off his balcony window, followed by
a familiar chuckle and a laugh. The dog ran down the stairs,
barking and pacing back and forth.

Rifle in hand, Pavlov cracked open the door. His cousin
was on the steps, hissing. She had been beaten and blood
seeped from her lips. Bruises covered her face. Pavlov went
back up to the top of the stairs, and his cousin followed him
into his living room.

When Pavlov asked what had happened, she leaned close
to his face, paused, took a deep breath, and in a barely audi-
ble exhalation, which he imagined to be the origin of her
demonic laugh, she uttered: I am pregnant.

He jumped up and went to the bathroom, ran water on
a hand towel and walked back to the living room. He covered
her forehead with the towel, and for the first time he noticed

her grey eyes. Hera the grey-eyed goddess, he mumbled to himself, savouring the line from Homer. Hera, he repeated to himself, a witness to the fallen Paris.

He looked her in the eyes, and she wept.

Pavlov walked to his uncles' house, and paced back and forth in front, rifle in hand. He stood below the front window and contemplated vengeance—death, followed by a cheap burial. He cursed his uncles, then edged closer to their front door and recited:

Death to those who dare lay their hands on a goddess's face. Death to those who turn bodies black and blue before death. Death will come to those who dwell in the abode of death. Death to those who refuse to set fire to the dead.

Death to the hands that beat the living dead.

The next morning, while his cousin was still asleep, Pavlov left the house and got into his car. Out of boredom, sadness and curiosity, he drove to the Bohemian's house. The Bohemian ushered him in and rolled a joint. Oily little brown balls of hash were chipped from a pasty roll, mixed with tobacco, carefully wheedled onto thin paper bound by spit, dribble and drool, eagerly lit, and slowly inhaled, with eyes closed. Then, through open mouths, exhaust was released, and lips shaped into smiles in anticipation of numbness, and forgetfulness of the mass killings of this world.

The Bohemian complimented the quality of the product. The best hash in the world, he said. One more reason for you to stay on here . . . Faddoul will arrive any minute, and you should meet the man who provides me with these exquisite herbs. A wild man, a wild man, a handsome, fearless man, a savage.

Pavlov replied that he knew Faddoul. Everyone knows Faddoul, he added.

A few minutes later, a man in sunglasses and a black leather jacket showed up at the Bohemian's door.

Pavlov despised Faddoul, a scumbag who still owed Pavlov's father for the burial of Faddoul's parents. Faddoul had refused to pay for the coffins and the funeral procedures. After his parents were buried, he went to Pavlov's father and complained about everything, even daring to accuse Pavlov's father of disrespect for his dead parents. Faddoul had fabricated one excuse after another. He claimed that he and his three brothers were insulted by the treatment of the cadavers. This, after all the work Pavlov's father had put into cleaning them, beautifying them and keeping them company before they were sent below. Faddoul had come to the house to complain, threatened Pavlov's father with a gun and left without paying.

As a kid, Pavlov had watched his father's humiliation, his mother's silence and fear. But when Pavlov had pulled out a knife that day, his father had calmly asked him to put it down. He remembered his father saying, with a hint of pride, A feisty little Spartan, my son, a feisty Spartan. It was then that Pavlov had become curious about the Spartans. He had read about them and their enemies, the Athenians. He had studied their gods and their wars, and finally in time he had read the philosophers. He vowed he would one day avenge his father as a Spartan would. But time had passed, and war had consumed everything.

Now, upon seeing Faddoul, Pavlov imagined himself a Spartan once more, spear in hand, cape hooked below his Adam's apple, wearing sandals and a sword, and a helmet that covered the cheeks and protected the eyes. I will burn Faddoul's city and enslave his wife and children, he thought.

The Bohemian introduced Pavlov, and Faddoul smiled and said that he knew the family.

I remember the funeral of your parents, Pavlov replied. Both your parents, he added, who mysteriously died on the same day. My father buried them with dignity.

Faddoul took off his sunglasses. He sat down next to Pavlov.

Yes, he said. My parents did both die on the same day. He smiled. But let bygones be bygones. I think we should all go for a drive. My car. I think we should go hunting birds. It's the season, he declared, and laughed loudly, filling the room with his smoky breath. And the son of the undertaker is welcome to join us. As a matter of fact, I insist that you come. Those who remember my parents, Faddoul said, will always be dear to me. That's the kind of family we are, my brothers and I always say.

Pavlov protested that he had been about to leave. But Faddoul was insistent, even holding Pavlov's hand, pressing him to come along.

The three men went down the stairs to the street and got into Faddoul's car. Faddoul had a smirk on his face. He clasped Pavlov by the shoulder and laid one hand on his neck. Tell me, does your father still own that building on the edge of the cemetery?

It's not for sale.

Faddoul burst into a loud laugh. You are a smart man. You see and know everything. You undertakers, you must have special powers, being so close to death. Have you ever seen the devil? People in the neighbourhood say they hear laughs and loud voices at night coming from the cemetery. Do you and your family host the jinn? He laughed. Our Muslim brothers on the other side of the city believe in the jinn. Maybe you've seen a jinn crossing from the other side into our cemeteries? He smirked again. If you do, shoot him for trespassing. It's a Christian cemetery, after all—or whatever remains of land in this region for these leftover Nassarah. He laughed loudly again, and the moustache on his upper lip formed a perfect straight line that mirrored his eyebrows.

When they reached the highway, Faddoul accelerated. Suddenly he turned to Pavlov, who was sitting in the passenger seat, and said, How is your fat uncle Mounir? Is he still fucking his brother's wife? I heard that undertakers fuck anything, dead or alive, anything that has a pulse or not. Did your father fuck his sister-in-law as well?

Pavlov imagined dragging Faddoul outside the car and stomping him into the ground. He eyed the gun at Faddoul's waist and thought about grabbing it, sticking it to his head and pulling the trigger, letting the car take its course, hit the wall and flip. He checked that the door was unlocked and the windows were down. That way, he thought, it will be easier for good Samaritans to pull the bodies from the car.

Faddoul saw him eyeing the gun, pulled it from his waistband and put it casually on the dashboard. Help yourself, kid. You seem curious about my piece. But help yourself to a cigarette first. And he laughed, then took the gun back, shoved it into his pants and accelerated, continuing towards the seaside.

The Bohemian, in the back, was amused by this boastfulness and talk of duels. Pavlov, he said, this is real life. People like Faddoul are rare in this world. He touched Faddoul's shoulders from behind. Faddoul, you are the real thing, he said, and Faddoul laughed and laughed, choking on the fumes of his cigarette. He glanced at the Bohemian in the mirror and winked at him.

I say never sit in the front passenger seat, Faddoul declared with a smoky exhalation. Let me tell you the story of my uncle. He was a gangster. I am talking the fifties here, long before the war. He hung out with these two badass criminals. All three of them *were* the real thing. We in my family were seriously rugged before and after the war. It didn't take a war to make us tough guys, we were hard as nails before any of the kids that parade around these days in their uniforms.

So my uncle and his partners had a dispute over money and women. The two criminals decided to whack my uncle. But do you know how they killed him? My uncle was sitting in the passenger seat. The driver grabbed my uncle's gun, and the man in the back stuck a knife in my uncle's neck. It was one of those old American cars with a low back seat, very spacious—they used to make them wide, and all leather inside. So wide, with a high roof, that you could swing a knife easily up and down, if you know what I mean.

Are you both comfortable? Faddoul looked first at Pavlov, and then at the Bohemian in the rear-view mirror, and both Faddoul and the Bohemian laughed sardonically.

They are laughing at me, Pavlov thought. What does it take to turn someone into a corpse? In his veins, he felt capable of killing, of causing death, of bringing death forth, recalling that tall figure who appeared to him in his dreams, always walking with a stick, swinging it and transforming the moving, the talkative, the affectionate, the sexually deprived and the sexually active, the greedy, invading, gluttonous omnivores into still, silent carcasses. Pavlov could call upon the tall man to hand him the cane now. In his dream, and outside of it too, he was capable of killing—he was sure of it.

As they drove nearer to the sea, they encountered an old pickup truck carrying birdcages. Faddoul tailgated the truck, and honked. Then he accelerated and drove beside it, waving at the driver to stop. The pickup pulled over. In the back were cages of chickens stacked on top of each other. The birds inside the cages looked stunned, nauseous and bewildered by the fast passage of the blurry world. Faddoul got out of the car, fixed his gun behind his back, pulled up his trousers and adjusted his belt. He walked calmly towards the driver and leaned on his half-open side window. He looked back at the Bohemian and smiled. Then he waved at the driver and asked him to get out and follow him to the back of the truck. The driver, half-defiant, half-concerned, adjusted his flip-flops, his short sleeves revealing where his left arm had been burned by years of dangling out of the window in the sun. His right arm looked pale and uneven by contrast. Everything was uneven about this man, observed Pavlov. One of his eyes was half-shut, he limped, and his hair, buffeted by the wind, had formed a disproportionate tuft on one side. What was more endearing was that he was aware of his unevenness, and before he got out to follow Faddoul, the driver fixed his hair, tucked his shirt in, straightened his head and shoulders. He walked around to the kept birds.

Faddoul pointed at the cages and asked the truck driver where he was headed.

To the slaughterhouse, the uneven man answered.

I need to buy a couple of birds, Faddoul said.

Faddoul and the man bargained and reached a price. Faddoul paid, and returned to the car with two birds tied together by their feet, hanging upside down in his hand. He threw them in the trunk and drove to a gas station, where he filled two plastic containers. On his way back to the car a splash of the liquid fell on his feet and he cursed. He tightened the lids on the containers and deposited the gas alongside the birds in the trunk, cursing and lamenting how he had ruined his expensive pants and shoes.

Now the car smelled of gas. When Faddoul reached for his pack of cigarettes, Pavlov took the matchbox and threw it out of the window.

Faddoul laughed and shouted, *Awake!* This man is always *Awake!*

They continued up into the mountains. There, they reached a remote area and took a dusty road that finally arrived at a dead end. This gave way to a secluded, errant plain.

Faddoul opened the trunk, grabbed the chickens in one hand and a gallon of gas in the other. He laid the chickens on the ground. Look how still they are, he said. But not for long. He poured gas on the chickens, and they fluttered, and then tried to jump—but the fumes of the gas must have made them too high and nauseous to do so.

Pavlov got out of the car and walked slowly towards Faddoul. Don't be cruel, he said.

Faddoul lit a cigarette and looked at the Bohemian then at Pavlov, laughing. He waved his gun in the air, turned to Pavlov and said, So you never answered me. Is your uncle still fucking his brother's wife?

The Bohemian was still in the car. Pavlov could hear him laughing nervously, entertained but clearly reluctant to join them.

Faddoul turned and flicked his lit cigarette down, and the birds went up in flames. They jumped in the air at last. He watched them, still grinning.

Pavlov, thinking of cruel, malicious, expelled gods, rushed at Faddoul and hit him from behind. Faddoul turned and pointed his gun in Pavlov's face. Pavlov could hear the jumping birds, and under his breath he recited a line from an Arab poet: *slaughtered birds that danced not out of joy but from pain.* The birds had come apart and they now started to jump towards the men like two balls of fire. One bounced towards Faddoul and hit his thigh. The residue of gas on his shoes caught fire, and then his synthetic pants and leather shoes burst into flames, and in no time his whole body was alight. He dropped his gun and danced with surprising grace, waving his arms and turning in circles as the flames caught the wind and rose up.

Pavlov heard the burning man laughing, perhaps even singing. He picked up Faddoul's gun. Faddoul stood in one spot and beat his body, flapping frantically, trying to extinguish himself. Then he waved his hands in the air once more and ran towards Pavlov, trying to embrace him. Pavlov aimed the gun at Faddoul and shot him three times. Faddoul fell to the ground, dead, the flames alive and completing their dance over his remains.

Pavlov turned to the burning chickens. They were exhausted and incapable of movement. He shot both of them.

Mercy, he said, mercy to all creatures.

He took off his jacket and used it to extinguish the flames surrounding the dead man on the ground.

Pavlov could hear the Bohemian's heavy, slow breath through the open window of the car, followed by whimpers of fear. He had rolled himself into a ball in the backseat and was glancing sideways at the scene with only one open eye.

Pavlov took the leftover gas and poured it over Faddoul, and watched his body go up in flames. The Bohemian was still in the back seat, trembling and refusing to leave the car, crying and hyperventilating. Pavlov took him by the shirt and pulled him out.

Stop crying, he said.

Don't kill me, don't kill me, don't kill me, the Bohemian pleaded.

I just saved you, Pavlov said. Why would I kill you?

But the Bohemian didn't seem to understand. He repeated his plea: Don't kill me.

You were planning to sell your inheritance to Faddoul. That was your plan. Pavlov gently pulled out the gun and put it to the Bohemian's head. He would never have paid you for your house, you know.

The Bohemian stayed silent.

What happened to your father?

The Bohemian cried harder. Again he begged Pavlov not to kill him.

Scumbags like Faddoul make you sign over your possessions then get rid of you on the spot. He would have killed us both and made it look like an accident.

I didn't know him that well, the Bohemian said.

I think you did. He excited you and took you out of your perpetual boredom. He seduced you. I just saved your unworthy life . . . What happened to your father? Pavlov asked again.

I don't know. My brother told me he threw himself off the boat.

I think you know, and your brother knows, that isn't true.

The Bohemian shook his head.

And your father? Pavlov repeated.

My father is beneath the sea. He killed her . . . My brother wanted him dead. At these words, the Bohemian wept even harder.

After a while, Pavlov and the Bohemian poured the other gallon of gas over the seats of Faddoul's car and set it alight.

They turned their backs on the burning and started the long trek down towards the bombarded city.

By the time Pavlov returned, Barbus was hungry and thirsty. Pavlov poured water into a plastic container and gave him food. The dog slurped and salivated and wagged his tail and ate. Then Pavlov walked the dog around the cemetery. Barbus sniffed the fence, picking up the odours of men, hyenas and the ghost of a fellow canine.

EL-MARQUIS AT HOME

The next day, Pavlov's cousin still lay on his sofa. Her stomach had grown into a visible semi-sphere showing her pregnancy. She helped herself to some of the food in the kitchen and ate all morning long. She walked barefoot on the old burgundy tile on the floor, stepping on its arabesque motif of strange flowers. She would periodically release chuckles, then suppress her loud laugh with food and drinks.

After she was full, she reclined on the sofa and stared upwards for the rest of the day, contemplating the white clay of the ceiling.

Late that night, Hanneh and Manneh knocked at Pavlov's door, weeping. El-Marquis is dead, they pronounced. His body is at his estate.

Pavlov grabbed his thickest coat and left his house. The windshield of his deathmobile was still broken and the doors had been marked by bullets, but it was functional and, he calculated, capable of transporting the now-still libertine on its rolling black wheels.

He went up into the mountains, following the tail lights of the two motorcycles, two dots illuminating the wandering lanes of Mount Lebanon. The wind entered the car, hit him in the face and filled his nostrils with the fresh cold air he liked. In time, he reached a large stone house that stood alone on top of a hill.

When Pavlov and his companions entered, they found two attractive cleaning ladies in short seductive aprons dusting the furniture and sweeping the floor of a grand salon. The women were singing cheerfully in French. A round chef was preparing food in the kitchen. He was masterly and clearly in control. A hairy Turk, thought Pavlov. Bald, short, with chest hair seemingly determined to overrun his ursine torso beneath his low-cut shirt. His arms were also unusually hairy, and ready to steadily invade the counter beneath his knife. He looked rough, but like the maids, he was singing, and his voice had a feminine lilt. When he turned to the stove, more hair sprang free from beneath his collar with no hesitation. A singing, cooking bear, Pavlov thought, and smiled to himself.

A long, thick rope lay in the centre of the salon beneath a pulley fixed to the ceiling.

In the bathroom, El-Marquis was resting, surrounded by ice, in a baroque-looking bathtub with four feet shaped like lion's paws. The paws were cast in gold. The scent of lavender perfumed everything from the marble floor to the French bidet that lay at the far end of the bathing space.

Hanneh and Manneh wept, and kissed El-Marquis' forehead.

Together they lifted El-Marquis, dried his body with thick towels, dressed him in a bathrobe and carried him into the study. They laid him on a long table. The room was filled with lilacs—El-Marquis' favourite flower, they told Pavlov. In the background, against the wall, was El-Marquis' imported Italian casket—a vibrant fuchsia with silver and gold handles. The edges of the coffin were covered with seashells. The long pole that passed through three handles on each side was shaped like a penis. The front of the casket was dotted with pink mosaic stones—a loud, colourful mosaic that from a distance revealed the shape of a vagina. The casket was to make an entrance during the evening, and it was the Marquis' wish to be transported in its beauty, then burned, at the end of the celebration.

Hanneh and Manneh gave Pavlov a purse filled with makeup. A black silk gown, men's soft Italian leather boots and a blond wig were laid out on a leather sofa. Pavlov requested cigarettes, a bottle of red wine with two glasses and a transistor radio with Rayovac batteries. Then he told Hanneh and Manneh to rest and come back in three hours.

I learned all this by watching my father, he said to El-Marquis once they were alone. It's stunning what we learn just by observing, isn't it? A different approach from your hands-on pedagogical style.

El-Marquis smiled sadly and agreed.

Now close your eyes, Pavlov said to El-Marquis. He washed the face, then dried it with a towel and began to apply eyeliner. Open your mouth, and take a sip of wine before I add the red to your lips, he told El-Marquis. He turned the radio on. A French tune by the Armenian singer Aznavour was playing, and they both hummed along.

Now, Pavlov said, this is where everything ends. There is nothing beyond these obsequies and these disguises. Are you ready to present yourself to the warmth of the flames and the omnipresence of ash and dust?

El-Marquis smiled, and Pavlov swayed and danced for a while.

Pavlov slipped the black silk gown on El-Marquis' body, pinning and tucking. The soft Italian leather boots came next. He combed the long blond hair of the wig and fitted it on the dead man's head.

When Pavlov was done, he nodded. He brought one of the bathroom's seven mirrors into the study for El-Marquis, and saw he was pleased.

Cigarettes burned in the ashtray. The music on the radio had turned to conversation.

El-Marquis faced the gold-framed mirror, then moved to the bathroom and faced another mirror and spoke. Pretentious mirror, fabulous mirror, narcissistic mirror, do tell, El-Marquis asked, who is the prettiest of them all? Who is leaving this pigsty behind with no regrets? Who made the best of it, and who is now looking his best?

A voice rose out of the abyss of the bathroom's drain and screamed back: Hideous boner, flat ass, crooked toenail, yellow-fever carrier, syphilitic mentor, bad singer, pretentious cunt, fag, lubricated asshole, saggy pouch of testicles, promiscuous orifice, fucker of students, monk's fart, menopausal hog,

degenerate, colonial subject, prostitute's rag, cheap mercenary, four-legged anilingus, cock devourer, bald, moist,
aged cheese, dried hummus, suffocating scarf, golden shower
on your face, silkworm, hairy gorilla, freak, bear, bottom,
capitalist, smudged feces, swallower of cum, fish-smelling
cunt, nihilist, bad dancer, drunk, needle junkie, failed poet,
assassin, filthy Bedouin, fascist mutt, existentialist je ne sais
quoi, shit, bastard, Stoic imposter, afterbirth from a stinky
whore, fascist, slavedriver, camel toe, fascist, fascist, fascist
chimp, dog, pig, goat fucker, mother fucker, daughter fucker,
slave fucker, sailor bugger, Bible papyrus to whip a donkey's
ass, camel jockey, one-eyed buccaneer, piss Zionist, soldier
of fortune, anti-intellectual ruler, vain bitch, meek, Christian
slave, hunchback's offbeat bell toll, orgasmic anus, impotent
ball juggler, pierced dick, dry well of lubricated old virgin,
wife-beater, Communist, masturbator, masturbator, masturbator, nun squirt on your face, pussy moustache, nymphomaniac
royal, shit eater, pussy licker, killer of anything and everything, everything . . . Human, ugly human, perish and rot!

The door swung open and let a burst of air in, and Hanneh
and Manneh entered. They began to weep again, marvel-
ling at Pavlov's talent for dressing the dead. And they complimented their friend, El-Marquis, one last time.

At the appointed hour, Hanneh, Manneh and Pavlov carried the body to the middle of the salon and laid it beneath a
large Christmas tree decorated with plastic penises and por-
celain vaginas. A rope was knotted around El-Marquis' chest
and neck, then passed up through the pulley. Hanneh and
Manneh worked calmly, and as usual executed their duties in

silence betrayed only by the clicks of their high heels. Hanneh supported El-Marquis, and Pavlov and Manneh held the rope. On the count of three, El-Marquis lifted into the air. In his silk gown, he appeared wrapped like an insect, suspended in the woven threads of a spider, swinging back and forth then spinning with the slow dizziness of an astronaut rotating in zero gravity or Jesus ascending at high velocity to the heavens. El-Marquis' polished leather boots projected, like a disco ball, random sparks of light on the marble floors and the surfaces of the walls. He had the hypnotized eyes of Russian royalty under the spell of a mystic. His blond hair cascaded past his shoulders, his fingers pointed downwards, his nose lifted upwards, his arms fell heavily, spellbound by gravity and hell. In time, the rope settled and the body hung calmly. El-Marquis was anchored, and he floated like a shipwrecked Moor in a dancing ocean.

There, Manneh said. He's risen.

Truly risen, Hanneh said with tears in her eyes, *hakan qam.*

Cars arrived, many cars, rich cars and poor cars. They filled the narrow driveway that led to the house. Men and women and every gender in between, in their finest attire, entered the house. Some wore disguises while others were nearly naked. Admiring words for the beautiful casket on display were voiced, and a jubilant atmosphere was immediately established. Loud music played, and drinks were passed around beneath the dangling body of El-Marquis. Two nuns in austere grey robes slow-danced in a corner, kissing and caressing each other's thighs, and four drag queens talked and drank champagne and waved their arms with flamboyant gestures. A middle-aged, bald crime writer immediately stuffed himself at the buffet, filling his plate with meat and seafood before rushing away to the dessert table.

When the dancing started in earnest, guests swayed around El-Marquis in a circle. A tall woman wearing a long black gown with a cut-out around her buttocks, exposing her anus, reached high and touched the hem of his dress, kissed it and wept.

In the opulent bathroom, people waited in line for the white cocaine provided by a dealer in a large cowboy hat and pointy boots.

Pavlov watched this timidly from the stairs that led up to the bedrooms. The mood intensified and an orgy began. He sat above and watched, with equanimity, the debauchery under El-Marquis' vertical body. He saw three men attached to each other, fucking like dogs in heat, screaming and moaning, their hips rocking with a tidal rhythm, releasing foul sounds from their orifices. He saw a woman lie back on a fuchsia sofa and spread her lace stockings as one guest after another ate her vagina and kissed her lips. On the other side of the sofa, a woman drank champagne, smoking and looking blasé, not judgmental but indifferent. Her exaggerated makeup, her fake hair, the high colour that covered her wrinkled neck, the extravagance of her dress and wild red shoes oozed wealth and an heiress's ennui with her massive inheritance and her life. A servant stood beside her, attentive to her every move, and at the slightest gesture from the woman this young man would lean his ear to her mouth and then rush off to give messages to a couple—a man and a woman—and another man, a dwarf, engaged in a threesome nearby. Following the heiress's latest directive, the woman lifted the dwarf and the man knelt on the ground and opened his mouth. The dwarf pissed in the mouth of the man while the woman screamed: *Rome, statue, fountain, a child, a pawn* and *a fish*.

Pavlov went outside and gave fire to his cigarette. He carried a bottle of champagne and slipped between the cars, away from the lights of the house, towards the road and down the hill. From a distance the house emanated warmth and the sound of singing echoed over the empty valleys.

The half-full moon combined with the light from the house led him away from the road until he found himself at the edge of a cliff. He stood there, and contemplated the possibility of flight. When should a body comply with the order to step forward and jump? How can the body subordinate itself with such helplessness to the mind? he wondered. Fear of existence, he answered himself. Perhaps the knowledge that everything in this world is to be feared is the only truthful state of being. But still, the question is: Do those who jump believe they are about to experience another consciousness, another self, or do they hope for absolute annihilation? The act of suicide must be, ultimately, the only path to emancipation, he argued.

He drank champagne and sat on the cliff's edge. He smoked and drank some more, and hoped for sparks of brilliance in the sky, but the closer light of the house dominated and abolished the possibility of all brighter visions. Ha! Man and his enlightenments! Pavlov said, and sighed. Too bright, too bright!

He slept on the edge of the cliff. He didn't feel the cold; he was too drunk to feel the mountain's frigid breeze or fear the certain presence of wolves and wild dogs. The noise, the lights, the fucking in the house must be repulsive, he thought, to the packs of animals howling in the valleys. Towards morning, he was woken by little bells, feeble and wandering, confusing in their arbitrary rhythms. To his ears, they sounded like competing chapels in the distance, sending conflicting messages through the tolling of their bells. He opened his eyes and saw goats passing by. Behind the animals was an old shepherd who frowned at him, his wrinkled face burned red by the sun. He wore a long coat, a wool turban on his head, and carried a large stick in his hand and an old rifle on his back.

The shepherd pointed up at the house and said, The devil lives in that house. Did you escape?

Pavlov didn't answer.

You must be too drunk to remember. That house is full of devils. I am on my way to the village and I'll be back with righteous men. Such men still exist. What took place in that house is evil. This land is holy and not for your kind.

When the shepherd and his goats departed, Pavlov walked back to the house. He grasped the handle of the front door and pushed to open it, but it didn't budge. He pushed again, but a corpulent, intoxicated body was obstructing it. He pushed again, harder, and the body moaned and finally rolled away from the door. Pavlov stepped inside. He imagined the shepherd peeking through the window, horrified by the sight. Nakedness was everywhere; bundles and clusters of flesh covered the floor, the chairs, the tables. No doubt the villager must have seen El-Marquis dangling from the ceiling, too.

A bearded man slept balanced on the edge of the bar, snoring loudly. Ties, shoes and shirts mingled on couches, drinks and bottles stretched across the floor, broken plates and broken glass were everywhere. One man's nose was bleeding profusely, but he was too unconscious or too drunk to notice. Another man lay face down, traces of blood on his bare buttocks. Pavlov looked around for Hanneh and Manneh. He walked through the salon, turning over bodies in his search. Finally, he found them in El-Marquis' bed. He woke them, and informed them of the old shepherd's threat.

Everyone should leave, Pavlov said.

The three of them cut down El-Marquis and put him in his casket. Then Hanneh and Manneh proceeded to bang on pots, waking everyone up and shooing them away.

Bit by bit, the party dispersed. Only the two nuns remained behind, begging to stay a little longer to fuck and pray, and enjoy the serenity of nature and God.

In the early afternoon, Pavlov heard vehicles on the road. He looked out the window and saw a tractor and three cars approaching quickly. Two men were perched on the sides of the tractor, hunting guns in hand. The cars were full of villagers with rifles. Their guns bristled through the windows, pointing at the sky. They came to a stop outside El-Marquis' house and poured out of their vehicles. The shepherd banged at the door.

The two ladies dressed as nuns opened the door, their large crosses gleaming on their chests. The men at the door stood stupefied, not knowing what to say.

The nuns addressed the men peaceably. Son, what can we do for you? said one.

How can I help you, my children? said the other.

The driver of the tractor stepped forward. We have been informed of sinful activities, he said, and of a murdered woman hanging in the middle of the main room.

The nuns cried out in surprise, and assured the villagers that they had been misinformed. The sisters had held a vigil all night. Whatever anyone had heard and seen would have been prayers and songs for the dead.

When the shepherd began to protest, one of the nuns stepped through the doorway onto the front step and said, My good Christian, whatever you saw was a vision from the devil in your soul. We will pray for you. Only God can forgive you for these evil thoughts. We will pray for you.

Who owns this house? asked the driver of the tractor.

A man who spent his life in America, one of the nuns replied. And now his wife has passed away. Let the family mourn in peace. The priest is on his way and we need to prepare for the funeral. May God bless you, my sons. Go in peace.

Bewildered, the villagers turned and left. But the shepherd lingered. He stood at the door, trying to peek behind the nuns into the grand house. Finally, he too turned and left, climbing into the last car and slowly driving away.

When night fell, Hanneh and Manneh helped Pavlov usher El-Marquis into the deathmobile. They drove back down to the outskirts of Beirut, the two motorcycles in the wake of the hearse, and then took the road towards the other side of the mountains.

At a checkpoint on the coast, a militiaman asked Pavlov if he had a body inside the coffin.

Yes, Pavlov said. The militiaman asked for the name of the deceased and the location of the cemetery. Pavlov gave him a random name—Kfartaba—and a village his father had once taken him to see.

The militiaman looked into Pavlov's eyes for a long time. My own family came from that village, he said. But I have never heard that surname.

Pavlov replied that he was taking the deceased to be buried in his wife's cemetery, which was in that village, because he was a Chaldean Iraqi without any other family in the country.

When the militiaman asked the wife's name, Pavlov took a risk and gave him a generic name, one that was bound to be in every Christian village. Khoury, he said.

The militiaman crossed himself and muttered, *Allah yerhamo*. He waved the deathmobile through.

Pavlov looked back and saw that Hanneh and Manneh had also been stopped by the militia. He pulled over. In the rear-view mirror, he saw the two taking off their helmets and letting their long hair fall loose. It seemed the militiaman had asked them to dismount. He and the two ladies exchanged words, then another fighter approached slowly. The second militiaman raised his M-16 rifle and aimed it at Manneh.

What came next happened swiftly, faster than the fall of Achilles' sword: Manneh pivoted and grabbed the rifle, Hanneh dealt the other man a blow to the face with his helmet. In seconds, both militiamen were on the ground, and the two motorcycles roared past the hearse at thunderous speed. Shots were fired towards the hearse and Pavlov dove under the seat. A jeep full of militiamen passed by Pavlov in the hunt for the two motorcycles.

Pavlov waited a beat, then drove towards the mountain. Half an hour later, two motorcycles appeared in his mirror and accompanied him along the serpentine road to the cremation house.

El-Marquis entered the furnace, and Hanneh and Manneh wept for three hours. When Pavlov gathered the ashes, he reassured them that the Society would carry out El-Marquis' last wishes. And with that, Hanneh and Manneh left Pavlov the money he was due, and kissed him farewell.

FLIGHT

Pavlov visited Florence, El-Marquis' old student, to give her the libertine's ashes as he had requested.

When Pavlov arrived at Florence's lavish apartment in Saifeh, the doorman swept him in and accompanied him up in the elevator, and then a maid in a blue apron and little crescent-shaped cap opened the door, her eyes downcast. Florence stood at the far end of a spacious salon, and waited for her maid to show Pavlov the way. Pavlov walked calmly towards her and extended his hand, but she turned away towards a large window with a view and asked him why he had come. Pavlov tried to reconcile the image in his head of her youthful self, as described to him by El-Marquis, with the woman who stood before him now. Florence fully looked the part of the bourgeoise, with her dyed hair, its streaks of blond breaking the homogeneity of brown, and her once-thick eyebrows that had been carefully thinned. The red paint on her nails, the heavy makeup, the French attire and pointy shoes—all of these reminded him of his father's mortician skills. She was surrounded by the platitudes of wealth: Persian carpets, ornaments, valuable objects and large paintings in thick gold frames.

Pavlov silently handed her the ashes in a plastic bag. She took it with the tips of her fingers, distancing its contents from her clothing with an outstretched arm. She carefully opened the bag, took a quick look and closed it immediately. She tossed the bag carelessly on a table and brushed her clothing, as if fearful some particle might have escaped and carried itself into her pockets or beneath her butterfly collar.

She poured herself a glass of wine and took a sip, eyeing the remains of El-Marquis with disdain. Then, brusquely, she grabbed the bag, turned and marched to the bathroom. She shut the door and before Pavlov understood what she was about to do, locked it with a click. When she reopened the door, the toilet's water tank was already refilling, and the bag in her hand was empty.

Florence burst into tears. He made me do things, disgusting things, criminal things . . . Here, you can keep your bag. I poured it all down the toilet. That's what monsters like him deserve. Now please leave, she said, and never come back here.

She called her maid.

Pavlov did not wait. He took the stairs, exited the building, and walked home with the empty bag. At the bottom were a few motes of dust, just enough to mix with Pavlov's own saliva and paste on his forehead. He walked to a secluded corner of the street, one that smelled like the urine of both man and dog, and danced. Then he threw the bag away and walked home with a mark on his head.

At home, Pavlov found his pregnant cousin sleeping, but Barbus the dog jumped with joy upon seeing him. Man and dog sat at the window and listened to the voices of the dead beyond the balcony. Do you hear the murmuring and all the talk? the dog said to Pavlov. They are eager to tell stories of their lives.

Yes, Pavlov said, I hear them all the time. Then he stood and shouted from the balcony, No one is important, none of you! There you all are, lying beneath the dirt, competing with one another, hoping to be remembered. Fools! he yelled, and the dog barked.

He lit a cigarette and blew smoke towards the stretch of stones across the road, and spat.

Fools! the dog repeated.

Dead fools! Pavlov echoed, and he danced.

The dog drooled and spat, and danced alongside him.

Then Pavlov remembered that his parents were buried in the cemetery, and he shouted to his father promises of liberation from the weight of the earth. For hours, and all through the night, he shouted and talked to the dead. After a while, he looked down and saw his teenaged cousin Pierre and his brute uncles and their wives staring at him. Then the brutes broke the door down and burst into his house and locked the dog in the bedroom. They gave Pavlov a beating—stomping on him and hitting him hard. Mounir would slap him and dare him to say another word, and Pavlov would mutter something, and a further slap would come his way.

The brutes threatened to take him to the psychiatric hospital if they heard him screaming profanity at the dead from his balcony again . . . Just like your mother, they said . . . Mad just like her.

In the middle of this beating, it occurred to Pavlov that his cousin Salwa had lost her laugh. She stood in the corner of the room, cursing her father, cursing her uncle and her brother. The dog threatened them too, growling from behind the door.

After finishing with Pavlov, the uncles grabbed the hyena by the arm and forced her home with them. You are a whore, they said to her. A whore!

HAPPY NEW YEAR, PAVLOV!

In early January, Pavlov went to visit the Bohemian, but he was not at home. He tried on two further occasions until, early one morning, when Pavlov knocked particularly hard on the door, the Bohemian answered.

The man looked rumpled and his nose was running. He didn't bother to wipe it. Instead, he sniffed constantly and manically tried to straighten his unkempt hair. His eyes were red, and he had clearly spent the night drinking and smoking. He had answered the door in his underwear, and when Pavlov entered, the house had the pungent smell of cigarettes mixed with unwashed feet and old, worn-down sandals.

He led Pavlov to the kitchen and said, Did you know that my mother was a loving mother, but she couldn't tolerate weakness? Yet she married my father, who was a weak man. Well, sometimes weakness is perceived as consideration and goodness. But weakness is selfishness. The greatest fear of the weak is extinction. Weak men fear death, because death excludes them from the grand spectacle of life. The weak are spectators and never participants.

A coward, my dear Pavlov, has a profound attachment to spectacle. The weak are curious souls who see life as a play. A spectacle, I might add, in which they don't have to participate, but only watch and assess. The weak want to witness the end of every story, but never want to face their own ending. What the weak ultimately desire is one spectacle after another. They have a childish dependency on entertainment, they are narcissists and fear the void of boredom, they need mirrors to make themselves exist. The weak, my dear Pavlov, are delusional, and they cannot comprehend the concrete.

My father was weak. What he admired most was the courage of others, the performance of others. He would go to church even though he was a closet atheist. He loved to watch the spectacle of pious worshippers, engrossed in their own subservience and slavery. He would come back and describe to us the people who kneeled, who climbed the stairs on their knees, who confessed, who drank the blood of Christ and then mingled it with their own. Do you know what fascinated him about Christianity? The elaborate rituals of sacrifice and the symbolic re-enactments of violence. He believed that society ought to appease its own inner violence by designating scapegoats. He was fascinated by the bystanders who stood and watched the flogging of two criminals and a rabbinical rebel who claimed to be the son of a God. He wanted to know: Who were these people who watched the Crucifixion? What were they wearing? How did they find out about this event? He would say that, if he had been alive, he would have followed too, eager to see the procession of pain and torture. Does that sound familiar, Pavlov? My father envied those fortunate people who stood on the sidelines to watch the flogging. He admired those spectators who spend their lives watching from windows and balconies . . . Over dinner, he would repeat the same words ad nauseam. What a scene! my father would say, what a scene!

He followed my mother every day and watched what she did. He would rush home from work just to be glued to her, and his biggest thrill was when she punished and beat us. He would stand still, pretending to frown, but he was watching, not feeling anything for our pain or suffering. He was hiding behind a mask of wrath, but really he was watching our mother acting. Do you know what she called him for as long as I can remember?

Pavlov took a drag from his cigarette and puffed smoke towards the kitchen ceiling.

Dog. She called him *perro*, which is Spanish for dog. It was only when she finally hit him that he bit back. He killed her because she ceased to be a spectacle. Because he refused to turn himself into an actor. Now, in his eyes, she had become real, not a spectacle. She had brought corporal pain to the spectator, to one of the mob, and now he, as the spectator, had turned into a sacrificial subject, against all rules of the game. She became death, his own death. There is nothing more visible than death. She was no longer useful to him because it was impossible for him to simply watch himself being beaten. He couldn't be on a safe, separate plane, watching. Corporal pain is disruptive to the gaze. She became death. She carried a stick, a broom, and beat him like a dog. So, yes. Death—and what better way to get rid of death than death itself, don't you agree, Pavlov?

Pavlov looked away.

Do you know why I take photographs? It's because, unlike my father, I deplore the narrative of spectacle, and the lies that come with it. When I take a photograph, I don't just stand there, neutral, and gaze. I am taking an action. With each click, I am cutting the flow of the spectacle into something still. Into fragments. I am shredding these human stories that are far too bloated with deceit and self-indulgence. Fragments, that's what I do. I hack away at humanity's delusions and I interrupt the long walk towards the cross. I shoot to abolish all beginnings and endings. Fuck this circus, I say. Let's reduce everything to little interruptions, like birds do when they cut the flow of a sky. We only kill each other to see ourselves as heroes in our fathers' stories. We tell ourselves stories that we can believe. I chose the medium that is the most disruptive to being a spectator. I render everything into slices of space and time. The world should become a series of unrelated histories, a collection of particles. We should deny the world its interconnectedness. Otherwise, we are nothing but a sick species who imagines that we are part of an eternal spectacle, a never-ending continuum.

I, dear Pavlov, unlike my father, am not a spectator. I slice up everything, all that he hungered to watch. My coward of a father deserved his own death. Once, I showed him a photograph of a boy mutilated in an accident, and all he wanted to know was if anyone had witnessed the moment of catastrophe. I told him, I don't know, I don't care, I don't remember. And he told me, But you were there! You were lucky. I ripped up the photograph and said, I was there, but I didn't notice the spectators.

I know you, Pavlov. They say you belong to a secret society, but I know you are alone in this world. You enjoy the warmth of cadavers. You are torn between the spectacle and participating in it. But you killed Faddoul, so I guess you're no longer just an observer. You are only half-delusional, and I admire you for that. Now, where are these falling bombs?

The Bohemian went out onto the balcony with his camera in hand. Let's stop their narrative of death, he said. Let's catch the bombs and stop them from falling.

For a few moments, he was silent as he took photos of the sky. Then he said, Pavlov, I want to become like you. I need to take action. I know these frozen images won't stop anything. Symbols are useless. I have some reassessments to make. I have to take action. One has to periodically change one's life. The illusion of the spectacle can only be stopped by exercising violence. In Christianity, the only moment of truth is when the Roman soldier's spear pierces the dangling heathen on the cross. I have to become that Roman soldier, my dear Pavlov. I have to wear a helmet, exchange my camera for a rifle and take part in the killing.

He turned back to look at the sky, but this time he did not raise his camera.

Two days later, the Bohemian joined the militia and was sent for two weeks of training in a camp on the outskirts of the city. Like all new recruits, he slept in a tent, was taught to dismantle and clean a rifle, and was warned not to shoot his peers from behind when advancing towards enemy lines; so many soldiers were killed in friendly fire, he was told. He learned how to crawl under barbed wires and to yell in response to orders. He was also instructed how to inject bullets into rifles and handguns, and shoot at a target from afar. The Bohemian proved to be an excellent sharpshooter. He was given a nickname, Abou Bohemia, by the trainer at the camp—but Abou Bohemia was repeatedly punished for insubordination. He couldn't sleep during curfew hours, he stole cigarettes from his peers' bags, he was caught masturbating in the woods, and in the showers he was caught staring at a fellow fighter's penis. Late the same night he was beaten while sleeping, under the covers of his bed.

But the Bohemian's marksmanship redeemed him. One night, he was taken to the commander's tent and asked if he was willing to kill. The Bohemian said yes without hesitation.

We need snipers, and that might involve killing everything and anything that moves. Everything is a target!

Everything is a target, Abou Bohemia repeated.

Every morning after that, he was trained on special equipment. The transition from the camera lens to the sniper rifle seemed effortless to him. During the rest of his indoctrination he managed to kill two snakes and ten lizards. He refused to shoot birds because, he declared obscurely, they were capable of migration and flight.

At the end of his training, he was taken to the front line. He met two sharpshooters, one by the name of Asswad, who had a permanent black ribbon on his forehead, and the other by the name of Abou-Aadem, or Father of Bones, because his specialty was shooting people in the tibia first to immobilize them. These shooters handed him a long rifle with a binocular that he immediately proceeded to calibrate by focusing on a discarded Marlboro cigarette package.

After this introduction, the shooters were sent to the sixth floor of an abandoned building. They settled in an apartment that, on one side, had a direct view of the ocean. On the other side was a hole in the wall where the snipers aimed their rifles towards the opposing faction in the city.

Asswad said to the Bohemian, No one should cross that road. No one. Not cars, not humans, not even a dog, nothing. You have to be diligent and patient and shoot whatever tries to cross that road. Now, we have three shifts here. Yours starts at noon and ends at eight. I am here at night and Abou-Aadem is a morning person. He likes to be here early, before he starts his job at the hospital. Here is something that you should be very careful about. Listen to me very carefully. This is a matter of life and death. Your shift takes in the sunset. Towards the sunset hour this house is lit up, because the sun hits it directly. During this time you must calibrate the binocular and not move. If you move, the light will go through the hole to the outside, and when you move back, your body will cover the hole again. So, tell me what happens, Abou Bohemia, when you move back and forth over the hole?

The hole will emanate a beam of light, signalling our presence to the enemy outside, and they could spot us. It would operate just like a light chamber. A sort of camera obscura, Abou Bohemia said and laughed.

I don't know what you mean by *obscura*, I don't know or care who obscura is, but bravo, you guessed it. The enemy is always watching for clues. They will know where we are hiding. So don't move a muscle at sunset. Cover the hole with your body and your rifle and don't move.

During his first sunset, the Bohemian looked over his shoulder and saw that the room shone with a soft orange light. The light cast rays of magenta and red that brought the Bohemian close to tears.

He looked at the wall behind his back and stood up and walked away from his gun and faced the large ball of fire that was sinking into the Mediterranean Sea. *Mare nostrum*, he said, and he wept and bade farewell to the light and to the ball of fire.

He walked back and put his right eye to the binocular. A bullet from the enemy flew towards the hole, through the binocular, and entered Abou Bohemia's eye. He fell on the ground, on his back, with one socket bleeding and the other wide open, witnessing the end of a day.

ALL THINGS CHANGE TO FIRE

The night after the Bohemian was buried in a modest grave, Barbus the dog awoke suddenly and began to howl. Pavlov's uncles' house was burning, going up in flames. Pavlov rushed out in the cold, barefoot, tripping on pebbles and mud. His cousin Salwa stood in front of the house with a biretta in one hand and the green-eyed priest's long-lost head in the other. She was screaming her loudest hyena laugh.

Pavlov tried desperately to enter the house to rescue his uncles, their wives and his cousin Pierre, but the wall of fumes prevented him. His cousin had poured gasoline in every room, on every floor. In the funeral home, she had saturated the wood and coffins and the chemicals used for the bodies. She had locked the doors from the outside and set fire to the house as she ran outside, half-naked, her round belly and her breasts exposed.

Pavlov screamed and she laughed even louder. She swung the priest's head in her hand and hurled it into the fire. Pavlov rushed forwards again, blinded, bewildered, shouting. The house blazed, while in the distance bombs continued to fall.

When it was clearly hopeless, Pavlov grabbed Salwa and went home, her chilling laugh echoing in the stairwell. She stood in his living room, almost naked, and he wrapped a blanket around her shoulders. Her belly was bigger now, and her body was covered with marks and bruises. They both stood at the window, helpless, and watched the house burn to the ground.

The next day, a jeep pulled up at Pavlov's door. Three militia asked to come in. Pavlov recognized one of them from the day he had retrieved Son of Mechanic's body from no man's land. He led them upstairs. They looked around, and informed him they were investigating the fire. They entered Pavlov's parents' room, where they saw his cousin and recognized her as the girlfriend of their comrade, the Martyr. They asked her to step outside with them.

Pavlov said from the doorway, without moving an inch, If you miss your dead friend, you can come and lay your hand on her belly and touch his baby.

The men were silent for a long moment. Then their leader nodded, and they left.

A week later, Hanneh and Manneh appeared at Pavlov's door. Salwa put on her shoes and filled a plastic bag with her few belongings. Pavlov gave her all the money he had earned from the Hellfire Society, and together they drove to the port. Hanneh and Manneh promised Pavlov that they would escort Salwa to Turkey before turning back. From there, she would go to Stockholm to join Pavlov's sister.

The boat sailed and Salwa, like a siren, laughed her way across the Mediterranean and into the Aegean Sea. A few months after her arrival in Stockholm, she gave birth in Södersjukhuset. She named her son Narr, the Arabic word for fire.

—

In time, Barbus the dog grew old and died.

Pavlov kept Barbus in his fridge for three days and three nights. On the fourth day, at dusk, he proceeded to excavate his father's remains. He carried the remains to the hearse and placed them beside the dog's body. Then he drove towards the cremation house high in the mountains.

On the way, Pavlov noticed a car following him. He confirmed his suspicion when he veered onto the rough road towards the mountain. The car followed him onto the small village road, closing the distance between them. He looked in the mirror and saw three men: the brothers of Faddoul. He drove over the hills, speeding towards the cremation house. He knew the terrain well, so he let the brothers follow more slowly on the narrow curved roads.

When he arrived at the cremation house, Pavlov quickly carried his father's remains inside. He opened the oven door and let his father rest there. Then he rushed to his father's old bed and pulled out the hunting rifle hidden underneath. He loaded it with bullets and went back out to the hearse to pick up the dog's body.

The brothers had arrived by then and were getting out of their car. Pavlov picked up Barbus and shot two bullets towards them. The gunfire took the brothers by surprise. They ducked their heads below their car doors and shouted at each other.

Pavlov rushed inside the house and reloaded his gun; and, dancing for his father, in tears, he lit the cremation oven. Then he took his gun, used it to break the glass in the nearest window, and held the brothers from advancing for three hours as his father burned. The battle was fierce and Pavlov howled and barked from inside the cremation house, jumping from one window to another as the brothers closed in on him, their pistols in their hands. In the last exchange of fire, Pavlov was hit just above his heart. He staggered back, wounded, to the cremation room. Holding his dog in one arm, he pulled the hose from the bonbon and gave it fire with his other hand.

First there was fire. Then there was wind. And then there was dust that rose from where the house had stood and spread into the valleys.

That night, echoes of a howl rose from the valley and up into the clouds, and towards the elsewhere of the stars.

TROJAN HORSE

The Bohemian, before his death, had told a fellow fighter about the killing of Faddoul by the son of the undertaker. He had also revealed the whereabouts of the body.

Faddoul's family had gathered up his burned remains and vowed to avenge the killing.

A week after the burning of the cremation house on the mountain, on the night of Faddoul's wake, Hanneh and Manneh picked up Faddoul's body from the morgue, laid it in a coffin and drove in Pavlov's hearse towards the garbage dump. There, they dumped Faddoul's body. Then they drove Pavlov's hearse to Faddoul's home.

Both Hanneh and Manneh had cut their hair and each wore a black suit. Manneh delivered the casket to Faddoul's family home for the beginning of the wake. When the family had gathered around the coffin, Hanneh leapt out of it, a pistol in each hand, and Manneh stepped forward from behind the open gate.

Blood flowed through the house and screams reached to the dark sky.

Manneh and Hanneh escaped through the back gate, got into Pavlov's deathmobile and drove it towards the seaside. There, they parked it and set it ablaze. Then they found their parked motorcycles and drove towards the mountains. They drove up Sanine mountain and then down shepherds' paths to reach the Bekáa Valley, and then they flew their machines in the direction of the west side of Beirut.

They stopped at a small hut to have a *manousheh* and drink Pepsi. Finally, they drove up to a funeral home. The sign on the door read:

Big Moustafa's establishment: Burial night or day. Our light forever burns.

We're here on behalf of the Society, Hanneh and Manneh called out as they entered. And they each glanced in the mirror and fixed their hair.

EPILOGUE

The war ended.

The house across from the cemetery stayed empty for years. Eventually, the cemetery was bulldozed and a three-storey building containing shops was erected in its place. The uncles' land was confiscated by the government under a legal loophole to expand the road, and because the uncles had neglected their tax payments, and later a mosque was built on it.

After many attempts by Pavlov's sister to find him, Pavlov was officially declared missing. Nathalie lived through many harsh winters in Stockholm and, after the death of her husband from a heart attack, decided to return to Lebanon to the house in the village. She turned her husband's butcher shop into a grocery, grew older, and eventually became sick and died in a home run by the nuns of the nearby convent.

On Nathalie's deathbed, one of the nuns came into her room and said that she knew what had happened to her brother. Pavlov's sister was breathing her last as the nun told her that her brother had set the cremation house alight and blown himself up. And, the nun added, the heathen deserved his hellfire. The final word Nathalie uttered was *fire*.

Pavlov's niece, Rima, came from Sweden during her mother's illness. Afterwards, she tried to sell Pavlov's house in the city, but Pavlov's death certificate was required. After engaging lawyers and experiencing gruesome Lebanese bureaucracy, with its corruption and expense, she at length decided to give up the legal procedures and returned to Sweden.

Years later, on a spring day, a young woman pushed open the door to Pavlov's abandoned house in Beirut and entered it. Over the course of a season, she hired Syrian refugees to paint the walls and repair a few necessities, in order to render the house habitable once more.

Ingrid, Rima's daughter, was in her twenties. She had long black hair, and owned a dog named Barbus Jr. Her favourite pastime was to sit on the balcony and read, smoke, drink beer from a bottle or, in the evening, have a glass of wine. She walked barefoot most of the time, and wore shorts and loose, translucent clothing. When summer came, she would often go up onto the roof and lie topless on a towel, sunbathing and reading. On weekends, a young man with a sports car would pass by and honk his horn, and she would disappear until the early morning hours. She would come back with high heels in hand, joyfully singing and dancing, often a little stoned or drunk.

One day, she heard a knock at the door and went to open it. The two women on her step asked if she spoke Arabic. She replied that she mostly spoke Swedish and English, and could understand some French, but had very little Arabic.

The women spoke to her in perfect English. They said they had come on behalf of the mosque across the street.

Ingrid invited the women in.

They were polite but hesitant, and insisted on staying at the door. Finally one of the women asked if she was the owner of the building.

This is my family's home, Ingrid said. I have the inheritance papers, she added.

The second woman said, We are here on important business. We would like you to ask your parents if the house is for sale.

I am not sure that we could sell it, Ingrid said. One of the owners, my great-uncle, is still officially missing and obtaining a record of his death is proving a nightmare in this country.

God willing, the sale could still be arranged, said the second woman. We have contacts in the government. There are ways around this issue. Many people went missing during the war. We all lost loved ones.

I rather like it here, Ingrid replied. I am thinking I might come here more often—or even move over here and stay.

The first woman seemed to hesitate. Then she told Ingrid that some people in the neighbourhood were complaining that her behaviour was immodest, and potentially offensive.

What do you mean, offensive? asked Ingrid.

The women replied that she was often seen sunbathing half-naked on the roof, and drinking alcohol on the balcony. She was heard playing loud music.

In my home, I am free to do as I wish, said Ingrid.

The ladies politely agreed with her. They assured her that they respected her Western manners, and her belief in another religion . . .

Or non–belief, Ingrid added.

We acknowledge that this is your home, and your life, the women said. But we ask that you be more sensitive to your surroundings.

Ingrid didn't answer. The second woman added, Your people are no longer here. They vanished, they moved away.

And some are buried here, Ingrid said. She gently closed the door.

That night, she played loud music and stood at the window, smoking and drinking a glass of wine. She stepped out onto the balcony and looked at the large cement structure across the street. She lit another cigarette and held its fire between her fingers. Then she blew smoke toward the sky, and danced above the cemetery road.